"Wiese deftly re-creates that magical, and all too brief moment in history when Bali stood poised between her timeless past and her touristic future, with old demons and new ones coming face-to-face across the frontier of myth."

Lorne Blair
Author, *Ring of Fire*

"This quality of book is rare, as are the rich insights of the author. He honors the culture and people of Bali with his writings, and he honors the reader with his integrity of expression."

Caroline Myss, M. A.
Author, *Anatomy of Spirit*

"Wiese writes truthfully and sensitively about Asia and Asians. Read it!"

Garuda Readings, *Garuda Airline Magazine*

"ON THE EDGE OF A DREAM evokes Bali as it was when it stood poised on the brink of entry into the modern era, when foreigners were still followed by crowds of cheering youngsters. Then as now Bali contained powerful magic. The gripping narrative brings to light the effects those strong forces exert on a pair of free-spirited Western adventure travelers in search of the marvellous."

Dr. Frederik E. DeBoer
Editor of *Bali Arts and Culture News*

ON THE EDGE OF A DREAM

ON THE EDGE OF A DREAM

MAGIC & MADNESS IN BALI

MICHAEL WIESE

Published by Michael Wiese Productions, 11288 Ventura Blvd., Suite 821, Studio City, CA 91604 (818) 379-8799, Fax (818) 986-3408, Homepage http://www.home.earthlink.net/~mwp

Editor: Geraldine Overton
Cover Design by Art Hotel, Los Angeles
Cover photograph by Walter Spies
Photos by Michael Wiese
Additional Photos by Geraldine Overton and Walter Spies
Illustrations by the painters of Sindu
Copyedited by Robin Quinn and Shyama Ross

Printed by Braun-Brumfield, Inc., Ann Arbor, MI
Manufactured in the United States of America

First Printing April 1995

For a catalog of other books by Mr. Wiese, please write the above address.

Wiese, Michael 1947-
On the edge of a dream : magic and madness in Bali by Michael Wiese.
p. cm.
ISBN 0-941188-19-1 : $16.95
1.Americans — Travel— Indonesia—Bali Island—Fiction. 2. Magic—Indonesia—Bali Island—Fiction. I.Title.
PS3573.I36805 1994
813'.54—dc20 94-35198
CIP

To the people of Bali
who opened my eyes to a new way of being.
I shall be forever grateful.

TABLE OF CONTENTS

1	Tibetan Seamstress	1
2	Got Nowhere to Run	7
3	Getting Some Religion	9
4	Splashdown	17
5	The Shadow Play	35
6	Learning to Speak	45
7	Fever of Dreams	51
8	Guardian Angel	63
9	Sindu Be-In	87
10	Temple of the West	97
11	Dogs of Bali	109
12	Trance Dance	129
13	Letters	141
14	To Make Our Demons Flow	151
15	Dance Fever	163
16	Painting Myself Into a Corner	169
17	Ashes, Ashes, We All Fall Down	183
18	The Children's Club	189
19	It's Taboo	205
20	It's Okay, I'm With the Band	217
21	Invitation to Trance	225
22	Payback	231
23	Offerings	241
24	The Volcano	247
25	The Return	263
26	Rope Tricks	275
27	Klungkung	289
28	Escape	301
29	Epilogue	307
	Glossary	313

Chapter 1

TIBETAN SEAMSTRESS

San Francisco 1969

It's midnight. Full moon. I stand at the back of the Chinese theater. The flickering light from the projector is heavily filtered through sweet-smelling smoke. Shadowy figures stand against the walls. Two thousand people dream together in North Beach.

On the screen, a rugged young man traverses a difficult mountain pass carrying a sacred scroll. A Tibetan seamstress floats above and whispers 'messages' on which he must rely or perish.

The audience is into it. My stomach churns. So much is at stake. We've been showing Midnight Movies here for a year, but never our own film. Until now. I want it to last. I want it to be over. I can't take it anymore, and go out into the lobby. Adrian follows, pacing back and forth.

Just then, the electronic music crescendos. The audience cheers. "We did it, we did it!" he cries.

The doors into the lobby burst open. I am suddenly adrift in a sea of feathers and fur. Bottles of champagne pop. Someone pours a bottle over my long hair, dousing my tie-dyed velvet suit. My friends from film school stand around and laugh. Joints are passed through the crowd.

This is a real 'coup.' We premiered "The Various

Incarnations of a Tibetan Seamstress," a twenty-five minute 16mm black-and-white student film, and the whole town showed up.

Most of the costumed audience has, is, or is about to partake of their hallucinogen of choice. Besides hippies and artists, the San Francisco society set is here, dressed in velvet, fringed leather and fish-net stockings, as well as opening-night gowns and tuxedos. It's the scene!

I spot Jean-Luc, the program director for the Cannes Film Festival.

"Well?" I ask.

"Fantastic, fantastic."

"Then you'll show it in the New Director's Program?"

"Of course, my boy, of course."

I get out a quick thanks before I am pulled away by Burt, a Montgomery Street financier. His face is red and puffy from drinking.

"I don't know what it all means, but they like it."

"You're not getting cold feet, are you?"

"Hell, no! I smell money. And when I smell money I move. Come and see me next week and we'll get the ball rolling."

"Fantastic, Burt, thanks."

Adrian comes up.

"Well? Don't keep me in suspense."

"Cannes is a done deal."

"All right! And the money?"

"Adrian, my lad....start writing!"

"Hey, this filmmaking thang is not so hard," Adrian says.

"Yeah," I say, my thoughts pulled elsewhere.

"Hey forget it. Besides, you're 4F if I've ever seen one. Come on..."

More and more people shake my hand. Pat my back. Pour more champagne. A blonde actress of Amazonian proportions appears.

"I am in your new film, aren't I? I've told all my friends it's about the power of the goddess."

"Yeah! Sort of..."

I give her a two-minute kiss until she has to pull away to catch her breath. I glance up. Sonny stands on the stairs to the balcony. She shakes her head and smiles, then flips me the bird.

Several members from the Jefferson Airplane and Big Brother have put together an impromptu band. A wave of psychedelic rock fills the lobby. A dancing frenzy carries me outside to the ticket booth which is decorated with Indian carpets and religious artifacts. The Chinese owner is counting the evening's take. He is very happy. He has seen our Midnight Movies "sold out" for the last year.

"Big night, Nick. You have much success."

At the end of a red carpet, in the street, are several klieg lights which splash light in the sky over Chinatown, North

Beach, and Nob Hill. What a night!

A group of white-faced mimes are dancing. Photographers take pictures of me and Adrian with our actors in front of the theater marquee. More champagne is poured by harlequin servers. There are jugglers, fire-eaters, and fortune-tellers who have been hired for the premiere. Rock musicians, drag queens, artists, and models pass joints and trade phone numbers.

Eddie, an old friend from high school, surprises me with a crushing handshake, smiling his irresistable smile.

"Hey! What are you doing here?" I ask.

"I got your flyer. You know I wouldn't miss your opening night."

"You still playing music?" I ask.

"Not much time with my studies."

"You didn't come all the way from Salt Lake..?

He nods.

"Still studying theology?"

"Trying to."

An assistant yells to me over the music that reporters from the *San Francisco Chronicle*, the *Haight-Ashbury Oracle*, and *Berkeley Barb* want a quick interview.

Hours later, about twenty of us are still partying through the North Beach after-hour bars along Columbus Avenue. Only a handful make it to Enrico's for an espresso at dawn. Boy, are we a tired mess.

I look like shit. All the better to beat the draft. This morning I have my physical at the Oakland Induction Center. Bummer.

Adrian paints on more makeup, "You're gorgeous," he says as he eyes his handiwork and laughs. "You look like our Tibetan seamstress!"

Chapter 2

GOT NOWHERE TO RUN

My stomach is in knots as I mount the stairs leading into the Oakland Induction Center. Hundreds of young men my age climb the steep steps, like lambs to the slaughter.

"Kill some gooks. Kick some ass."

These macho punks actually *want* to go to Vietnam. There are no others like me. Maybe they're already in Canada.

We are herded into a green-walled classroom to fill out forms. It's claustrophobic. The men sit at tiny desks like school kids and horse around as they complete their applications. Cigarettes dangle from nearly every lip and fill the room with the exhaust.

These guys have never seen anything like me. I try to ignore their wisecracks.

"Does the queer want to kill some gooks? Kick some ass. I'll kick his ass."

Screw them. The more of an outsider I appear, the more the doctors will see that I don't fit in. My goal is simple. See the psychiatrist. Get out.

I'm told that if you don't wear underwear, they'll assume you're gay and send you straight to the shrink. Watch this. Fifty of us stand in a circle. A red-headed, fat Sergeant commands us to "drop trou." Here goes...

"Get that faggot outta here and away from my boys,!" screams the Sergeant to an assistant. I'm yanked from the room and hurried down a hallway to the shrink's office. All right! I'll be a free man in no time!

I hand my doctor's letter to the shrink, who looks it over then sets it down. My pitch is real short.

"Listen, the quicker I'm back in the street the better for everyone. These losers can throw their life away. They don't know any better. Me, I've got important things to do."

The ashen-faced shrink is inscrutable, like the Sphinx.

"Besides I have allergies and mental problems." There. I said it.

The shrink says nothing. He stares at me for a moment, then resignedly leans forward and stamps my papers: 'Fit To Serve.'

"Welcome to the Army," he smiles, self-satisfied.

Chapter 3

GETTING SOME RELIGION

Hong Kong. An hour before midnight. It's far too hot to sleep. I climb into a colorful rickshaw pulled by an incredibly strong old man. On the panel above the footrest is a painting of a space capsule landing on the moon. The driver turns around while jogging.

"You American? You go to moon?"

"What?"

"You go to moon?" nodding to the night sky.

"No, no. I go to night market. To meet my friend."

I lift a bowl of noodles. The hot broth is fishy and steams my face. There is a string of small lights above the street vendors stalls. I watch the action. People come and go, to and from work. Doesn't anybody sleep here? Wave upon wave of bobbing heads as far as the eye can see pass by. Then, suddenly there he is.

A blonde-haired, aristocratic face floats among the throng of Chinese faces. White shirt buttoned at the top, black pants and sandals. The light reveals his ruggedly handsome face as he talks animatedly to someone beside him. When he gets closer, I don't see anyone. Maybe he's talking to himself.

He sees me immediately and gives me that famous nod and raised-eyebrow wink. He makes a beeline to the noodle stand. He shouts an order in Chinese and sits down beside me, bright and beaming.

"Eddie! Jesus, you actually did it."

We give each other a hug. Then another.

"Damn, I'm really glad to see you."

He gives me that irresistable smile.

"I couldn't resist your invitation. Has it been difficult for you? The draft board and all?" he asks.

"No, not really, I keep to myself mostly, taught a bit of English."

He starts rolling a cigarette on an old rolling machine.

"Want one?" he inquires.

"No thanks, I don't smoke that stuff."

"Me neither, I just like making them," he laughs.

"So, how long have you got?" I ask, nudging him.

"Only a week. Then I'm suppose to go back and take my exams."

"You don't sound too enthusiastic."

"Yeah. I'm not sure I want to be a missionary."

We walk along the shoreline and look at the fishing boats. Back in high school in Indiana, Eddie and I were best friends. We even started a band. He had great hands with long fingers and a great sense of rhythm.

"Remember the Esquires? And how we had to sneak you out of the house to play those dives along Route 45?" I ask.

"Yeah, until my dad showed up at Ducey's. And that was the end of that," he laughs.

Eddie's father was a very strict guy. He was a brilliant scholar and theologian who taught Hebrew and Greek at the University. He pulled the strings to get Eddie into the theology program in Salt Lake. Now Eddie wants out.

"And so what are you going to do," I ask, "if you're suppose to go back in a few days?"

"I'm going to do what I want to do."

"And that is...?"

"Something important."

"I can dig it," I say.

Eddie and I hang out together for a few days. I never thought one day we'd be traveling together. He's spent most of the 60's in a seminary following his fathers footsteps to save pagan babies, while I was in San Francisco becoming one.

He moves into my hotel. It's cheap but relatively clean. We share a funky bathroom at the end of a hallway. One night, sitting on the balcony and looking out across the rooftops and shop-lined streets below, listening to the night sounds, we spot three tall women in slinky silk dresses looking up at us, trying to get our attention. There's electricity in the air. Eddie spots them first.

"Look there."

"Beautiful."

"Hello, hello, " they shout.

"Come on up," I yell.

There's something fascinating about them. The girls come up, and lean against the wall, smoking cigarettes. No one speaks, we just all eye each other. Eddie keeps stealing glances at the very beautiful thin one in the red dress. She looks Thai or Malaysian. Long straight black hair, beautiful black eyes and skin, small breasts, big arms and wrists.

He can't take his eyes off her.

And she can't take her eyes off the handsome (and to her, rich) American. Eddie sits very still, not moving.

The girl leans next to Eddie and rubs her leg against his arm.

Eddie abruptly stands up and stuffs his hands into his pockets.

"You think me pretty? You want see more?" She pulls back the red silk, showing off her thigh. Eddie backs up, smiling slightly.

The other girls smile, as the seduction mounts.

I stand.

"Eddie, I'm going for a walk. She's all yours."

"No wait. Stay," he laughs.

"No, Eddie, they're not my style." I pucker my lips and throw the girl a goodbye kiss.

"What's matter, you no like me?" the girl says.

I laugh.

"You no make joke me." Her raspy voice deepens.

Eddie is startled.

The girl shoves me hard against the wall and turns to Eddie.

"What's matter? You no like make boom-boom? Good boom-boom. Cheap price. Stupid guys!"

The girls turn away and shout insults back at me and Eddie.

Eddie is baffled. I don't think he's ever seen anything like this before.

"Good drag, huh?"

"Yeah...I thought...you know...Jeez."

Late one afternoon, we wander through the back alleys searching for a restaurant. The streets are backed with people and rickshaws and delivery trucks. Some beautiful hostesses smile at us, then we go down some steps into a night club.

"See that! Women are always giving us subtle messages. If we don't pay attention, we'll miss the signs. I was going to do a film about that in San Francisco. I was this close to having the money."

"And do what?" asks Eddie.

"A film. A film about women. I was going to call it 'Messages, Messages.' I had women all over me wanting to be in it."

We squeeze through the crowd. Eddie stops at a restaurant with a large statue of Confucius in the window. He throws out his hands.

"Confucius says, 'he who make decision, has happy life'."

He smiles that smile, keeping me in suspense.

"What have you decided?"

"Let's make 'messages, messages' together! In Bali!"

"Bali?"

Before I have time to consider the liabilities in his proposal, we've pooled our money and bought a CanonScopic movie camera and a tape recorder, and we are on our way to Bali.

Chapter 4

SPLASHDOWN

Clambering children thrust jackfruit and small carvings into my face through the open window of the bus. Several chant "*minta wang, minta wang*" over and over like madmen as they dance around us, holding out their hands. We climb out. So this is Bali!

Eddie and I push away the hawkers and find ourselves in a dusty lot. Jesus, it's hot. It's so bright that I can barely keep my eyes open. The air is filled with sweet and pungent smells, incense, and our own two-day-old funk. Nearby are drink stands with rickety wooden benches. Gaudy billboards with large orange Indonesian letters advertise "KRETEK."

What a long bumpy ride! I stretch, trying to get the kinks out of my body, and then I sit down gingerly. What little butt I had is now gone—bone against plank. I'm beat, but excited. The newness gives me a rush. Everything is so stimulating. I know great things will happen to us here.

Eddie is wired and ready for action, as if powered by a dozen extra batteries. He was never this wired back home. He says it's the air. A couple of young boys rush up.

"Darimana? Darimana?

Market urchins with something to sell. We don't understand. They shout louder. Maybe they think tourists will understand if it's louder. Fat chance.

"Ubud, Ubud, Sanur, Sanur, Kuta!" shout the urchins. We hear these destinations for the first time. We follow a pencil-thin kid who offers, "You go beach? Kuta? Okay. Okay. Come, come!"

Why not? We toss ourselves and our camera gear into a badly dented *bemo,* a truck with two long benches in the back for passengers. There are so many people crammed into this small, covered-seating area that I don't believe it will really hold us. The kid stands on a small platform holding onto a handle, and off we go. A breeze blows through the open sides of the bemo. Twenty minutes later the road dead ends at Kuta. There's not a soul on the beach.

Eddie and I walk past the mud-walled, thatched-roofed houses of Kuta village. It's hot. Really hot. We stop under the shade of a banyan tree. There's a dried-up offering on the ground.

A stucco guesthouse or *losmen,* rests under some coconut trees. The beach begins at the front door. A hand-painted sign says "homestay." It has eight rooms. Only half are filled. It costs about 50 cents a day and includes banana pancakes and tea for breakfast. At this rate, my $300 will last for over a year.

A mildewed, dirt-floored room is our new home. There are two stained and sunken mattresses on handmade wooden frames; between them is a single oil lamp on a bamboo table.

Behind the table is a chicken wire window with holes you can push three fingers through. That's not going to stop any mosquitoes. Outside is a view of coconut trees and the ocean beyond, with row upon row of white caps. Inside, the walls are filthy green paint. A small room doubles as shower and toilet. There is one hole in the floor. No door. I surprise a fat lizard who slithers through a crack.

Eddie puts a small statue of Jesus on the table.

Ragged French travelers and Australian surfers occupy the other rooms. They shout and yell as if they own the place.

The smell of dope permeates the air. A dollar buys a week's supply of potent Thai sticks. I get Eddie to try some. Big mistake. He laughs hysterically for hours and then gets paranoid and sees "the evil eye" everywhere. He must feel guilty for 'straying from the path.' We can't get off the beds for the rest of the day. In the morning when we wake, we swear off dope off for the rest of the trip. We'd rather see Bali.

Rock and roll from the next room drowns out the gentle whispers of wind blowing through the coconut trees outside our window. A sun-fried, topless French girl stands outside our door and reports that Mick Jagger is at the Bali Hai Hotel.

"Mick Jagger, he's so cool," she says to her bearded surfer friend on the other side of the wall.

"Let's go see him!" She sings off-key, "I can't get no... SATISFACTION!"

Eddie says, "I'll give you some satisfaction."

"She's got a boyfriend, Eddie," I tell him.

"So?"

The Bali Hai Hotel is half an hour away in Sanur, a beach on the opposite side of Bali's southern peninsula. Mick Jagger?

It reminds me of the Rolling Stones' concert in Altamont. Someone was beaten to death by the Hell's Angels. Whatever happened to love and peace? Suddenly, people around me were getting killed, at home as well as in Vietnam. It made no sense to stay. I'm glad to be here.

We stuff our things under the bed and padlock the door with the world's smallest lock. Within seconds Eddie and I are on the beach.

It's so bright I can hardly see. The sky is magnificent. The air is warm and clean. I walk between the brightly painted fishing *praus* and under the hanging fishing nets, which cast beautiful soft shadows on the sand. The water is pristine. I float. The warm water heals me

Eddie runs into the surf laughing, and then tackles me in the water and dunks my head under three times. "With this water, I anoint you in the name of the parrot, the lizard, and the banana pancake."

Later, half-exhausted, we collapse on the beach.

"It's going to be great here," I say, as I rest my head on the warm white sand.

We see a group of people gathered ahead and go to

investigate. Reverently we approach, as Balinese women bring offerings to two priests. (I get a great shot of the back-lit halos that encircle their heads as they carry the offerings.)

"Oh, man," is all Eddie can say, over and over, as the women pass. We're mesmerized.

There is incense stuck in the sand, surrounded by half-coconut shell caps filled with holy water and flower petals. Behind us, a small walking *gamelan* group with a few gongs and drums knock out syncopated patterns.

Some boys ready a small *prau*, a Malay sailing boat with only enough room for about four or five people. A priest, carrying a large woven basket, wades through the water and then climbs into the boat. The boys paddle like crazy through the breakers. They stop about 50 yards offshore.

The priest sprinkles some holy water from a pitcher over various objects, then throws them into the ocean. I can't make sense out of any of it. Then the priest pulls a duck from the basket and throws it into the air. The duck flies for a moment, but then with a stone weighted to its foot, it crashes into the water and is pulled beneath the waves. Just then a boy dives in and retrieves the duck. Some of the floating offerings are gathered up, and the boat returns to the shore. I walk closer to see.

Some of the offerings are cigarettes, flowers, and carved palm leaves that have been cut and folded together in quite beautiful patterns. I pick one up and put it my pocket.

It's not long before Eddie wants to trade some cigarettes for the duck and the coconut bowls that were retrieved by one of the boys. What are we going to do with a duck?

Back at the homestay, Madé Gitah, a souvenir salesman, hawks some Balinese paintings. He sees us and rushes up.

"*Darimana*, tuan?"

"What's this darimana stuff. Everybody's always saying darimana. What's it mean?" I ask.

"Where are you from?

"Where are you from? I reply.

He smiles.

"We're from America."

"Ohh, America. You go to moon?"

He shows us a few of his paintings. Eddie picks one up. Sensuous women sell fruit in the marketplace and steal looks at the men out of the corners of their eyes.

Eddie is fascinated. "Are Balinese women really like that?"

Others are underwater ocean scenes of horrible, large-fanged sea monsters. No wonder the few Balinese that are fishermen spend a lifetime throwing offerings into the sea.

Madé explains that offerings are made to both the gods in the mountain and the demons in the sea. The Balinese orient their beliefs around *Kelod* (the direction toward the sea) and *Kaja* (the direction toward the volcano). It's a cosmology structured on high and low. Humankind is balanced in between. Madé says he doesn't like to come to the beach because there is lots of black magic. Oh, terrific. And the beaches are where the travelers hang out.

Eddie asks, "If you don't believe in black magic or demons, can they still get you?"

"I don't know."

I pick up one of the offerings I brought from the beach, and reverently place it at the entrance to our room.

"Feel better?" I ask.

He crosses himself theatrically.

"Now I do."

We all laugh.

Madé leaves as it starts to pour. The rain beats down for about an hour and then all is still. Night comes early and with it cool ocean breezes. I prop myself up in the bed and write a few letters by the flickering light of the lantern.

Dear Sonny,

I'm sorry how things turned out. I couldn't stay and face the draft. I'm sorry I couldn't keep up my side of things. I guess a lot of people are a little more than disappointed in me.

Now I've got a lot of learning to do. And Bali's a good place to do it.

In any case, I'm not the guy you once knew. I am stripping everything down to the basics and starting all over.

Love, Nicholas

PS. Please destroy this letter after you've read it. I'd hate the draft board to know where I am.

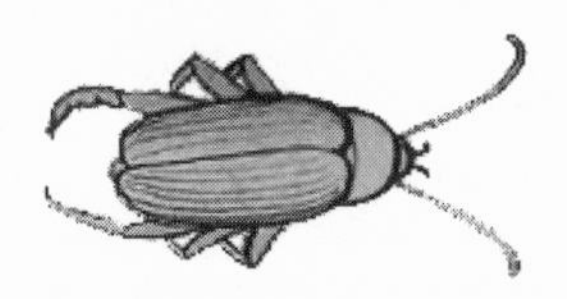

In the morning, we are up early. We can't wait to explore the market in Denpasar—Bali's main city.

The light is exquisite as we pass the rice fields.

"Oh man, is this ever great," Eddie says and swings his suntanned body outside the back of the *bemo.*

He shouts and sings Handel's *Messiah* with absolute joy. I love that about Eddie; he doesn't hold back. He motions to me to join him, and I hang out the other side and snap some pictures. The other passenger (an old farmer with a bale of cane) doesn't know what to make of us.

A truckload of young soldiers passes us. They look down from the truck and glare at us. They wear green uniforms about two sizes too small and carry old rifles. I wonder if Vietnamese soldiers look like that? Very intense. Even scary. I wouldn't want to mess with them.

The muffler-less bemo sounds like a chain saw ruining the tranquility of the countryside. Talking is pointless. White exhaust fumes curl up and around the back of the bemo, forcing us to sit down and cover our faces. The roads are filled with potholes after the rains.

Bam! Bam! Kabam! If there were ever any shocks on the bemo they're certainly gone by now.

We are green with nausea by the time we arrive twenty minutes later. We get out. Eddie sticks his fingers down his throat and throws up his banana pancakes.

"Try it, you'll feel better."

He's right. The cold clammy feeling passes, and I feel great. Great to be in Bali.

We walk around Denpasar to get the lay of the land. The city is terribly congested. Bali is just as crowded as Java, with about 2 million people crammed onto an island the size of Delaware. We can't wait to visit the three towering volcanoes in the middle of the island and to walk across the fertile green rice fields.

Today is market day. Push or be pushed, we make our way through the crowded market. Village women display jackfruit, *durian*, oranges, mangos, papaya, bananas (a dozen varieties), coconuts, lemons, and pomegranates. Eddie walks through the market surreptitiously squeezing the fruit and eyeing the women. We are hot and sweaty from the heat.

There are heaps of herbal concoctions that boggle the imagination. A polluted river next to the market sends up an unbelievable stench. Several women stand at the side of the river, pull back their sarongs, and relieve themselves. Jeez! We're talking funky. Packs of semi-wild Bali dogs scavenge and fight over the remains.

I want to get a sarong. We buy several but we're not sure how to tie them. A market hag with red, betel-nut-stained teeth cackles as she carefully folds then ties mine. Looks pretty good.

Eddie buys some *kreteks,* Indonesian clove cigarettes. We each light one up.

"These aren't real cigarettes, more like candy cigarettes," justifies Eddie, who doesn't really smoke. They give off a wonderful scent which permeates your clothes all day.

Denpasar has gone cosmopolitan. The government workers prefer white shirts and black trousers, which they think give them a modern look and the right to look down on sarong-clad farmers, craftsmen, and food vendors. We strut along in our purple and orange sarongs. Power to the people.

We come to a large open field, a square in the middle of town. On the other side is the Denpasar museum. We enter through a large gate. Inside are two large, masked ritual creatures. One is a very frightening woman with bulbous eyes, fangs, long fingernails, and a long red tongue. She's covered in hair. The other is a kind of lion creature like those you'd see at Chinese New Year.

A guide comes smiling, "*Salamat pagi*, darimana tuan?"

"Salamat pagi. Saya dari Salt Lake City," replies Eddie confidently.

The guide speaks no English but we come to understand the two creatures are Rangda and Barong. Lining the walls of the museum are displays of shadow puppets and magic kris (daggers). I wonder whether this stuff is old or still used in Balinese ceremonies.

We stop at a *warung* (tea stand) in the street for some high octane *kopi susu,* which is essentially raw coffee grounds in a glass of milky hot water. I've learned that if you let the grounds settle to the bottom of the glass *before* drinking, you won't have to spend the rest of the day picking coffee grounds from between your teeth. It's pretty powerful stuff. My stomach starts to gurgle. I look around for a toilet, but there's nothing in sight.

A crowd starts to gather around us. Knowing he is being studied, Eddie pulls out his cigarette-rolling machine, and begins a performance. With every move, the audience grows bigger. Concentrating intensely, Eddie begins by opening the tobacco pouch and religiously rations out its contents into the machine. He delicately takes the white rolling paper from its package and gently lays it in the slit in the roller. Next he exercises his fingers until they are ready to twist the machine, which eventually births a cigarette. Continuing, he then slowly raises it to his lips, lights it and savors the taste before exhaling the smoke. The audience coos with every move and cheers on the exhalation. Eddie loves making a spectacle.

When we are ready to leave, a mob follows us.

"Hey, man," I say, "this is kinda scary. Now I know how the Beatles must feel."

Eddie and I walk faster and faster. The crowd follows. Kids shout, "*Minta wang, minta wang.*" (Give me money). We start running. Several dozen crazed young men chase us. It's getting out of hand. We're sprinting now. We duck into a funky tourist restaurant. A toilet at last! The crowd disperses.

I look at Eddie. "That was close."

He is sweating like crazy and he's out of breath. So am I.

"What do you think they would have done with us,?" he asks between pants. He makes a face and we can't hold back the laughter.

We tuck in our shirts and smooth back our hair. The smell of chicken saté gets Eddie's attention. We look around and see we are at The Three Sisters. A sign shows it's famous for its magic mushroom omelets. Three vivacious siblings run back and forth taking orders and delivering food.

We order *nasi goreng* (fried rice) and *mie goreng* (fried noodles and vegetables), saté, and more coffee.

This is obviously a popular hangout; between the flirting and socializing, it's the place to be. There's not much to it: cobalt blue tables with benches, a coffee-tin can stuffed with dirty forks, and paper napkins. There's a seedy, but necessary pit stop like this in every Asian city where unofficial information is shared between travelers.—where to stay (cheap, cheapest, free), buy dope and/or sex, extend your visa, or learn what's happening in Thailand or India. I like to go to these places for a day or two, compile information, and then get off the beaten path.

Eddie isn't comfortable here with the other foreigners. Bali is *his* discovery. Everyone else can buzz off. Period.

Eddie is still hungry and orders second, then third portions of everything and eats with a ravenous appetite. He can really put it away.

Several teenage boys are hanging around the table marvelling at how much Eddie can eat.

As he finishes, a big, bearded guy steps through the crowd and sits down at our table and introduces himself. "Ida Bagus."

"I'm bagus, too," I say. ("Bagus" is Indonesian for good.)

"No, I'm Ida Bagus. That's the name my Balinese father has given to me," he says with a heavy Swedish accent.

Whatever. I call him "Big Swede" for short. He is very tall and thin, with long hair and eyes filled with experience. I'd guess he's about forty. He's a righteous vegetarian and wants everyone else to give up meat too. He orders three plates of food as he divulges his big discovery.

"The Balinese are the healthiest people in the world," he tells us. "They live to ripe old ages because they can't afford to eat hamburgers."

He's been traveling for twenty years and now lives in Bali. A rule of the road is that the longer you're away, the hipper you are. (I've been in Asia over a year, Eddie only a few weeks.) That makes "Big Swede" top dog. His passport is filled with dozens of expired visa stamps. Morocco, Pakistan, Istanbul, Afghanistan, Nepal, Thailand, Cambodia, Hong Kong, Sumatra. It might as well be an Olympic Gold Medal. In twenty years my passport will look like his.

Two Javanese girls in halter tops that barely support their mango-shaped breasts sit down on the bench on each side of Big Swede in front of their plates of food. One of the girls reaches down into her bag and pulls out a hairbrush. We can't take our eyes off her. From our vantage point, we can see where the brown tan line meets the pale skin and pink nipple.

The girls braid his hair and fondle him.

"My tantric experiments. They'll do anything for me. We balance our energies, don't we?" he says, as he pats one on the butt and laughs.

Eddie, who is sheepish and silent, rolls another cigarette and covertly blows smoke towards the Swede while eyeing the girls. Big Swede proclaims that Kuta Beach is one of his favorite places. "Pure, untouched."

Putu, one of The Three Sisters, brings me the bill. Big Swede ignores it until I point out that everything delivered to this table is totaled together.

"Hmm, give me 10,000 rupiah. My money is at the beach."

I hand it over.

We all catch a bemo and return to Kuta. When we get off the bemo, we are greeted by a familiar face.

"Hallo, my name, Madé Gitah, you want to see my paintings?" Swede grimaces and waves him off.

"That Sindu village stuff is crap. You want to see good paintings, go to Penestanen near Ubud," says Big Swede.

Big Swede is staying with the girls in a rich friend's bungalow further down the beach. He suggests we walk with him. Eddie trys his Indonesian on the girls. They laugh.

I join Big Swede. The girls wade in the surf. Their sarongs stick to their shapely little butts. Eddie follows. The girls wade out waist deep and dance teasingly for Eddie.

Big Swede smiles, "There's only two things worth worshipping: women and God. In the Tantra, when you join with a woman you are joining with God."

I know what he's trying to say. I'd like to express something like that in my film about women.

"It's kinda like they are muses," I add, but Swede's not paying attention.

I take a few pictures of the girls dancing. When we reach the bungalow, the nymphs say goodbye and run inside. Big Swede tells us he'll see us later.

We walk on further toward the peninsula which juts out into the bay. (Hey, he forgot to pay me back!)

I feel incredibly free. No worries at all. My mind is clear. I am alive and happy. This is exactly what I've always wanted. In San Francisco, everyone talked about going out into the world but no one I knew ever did.

Chapter 5

Wayang Kulit
THE SHADOW PLAY

It's night. I've missed the hashish-enhanced sunset, the main event on Kuta among the homestay crowd. We spent one evening with them. Mostly Australian surfers and loud rock and roll. All they could talk about was the waves.

Ketut, the homestay manager's son, waits by the door. He's Eddie's friend and has been teaching him Indonesian. He invites us to go to a ceremony in nearby Kuta village, and he loans us each a brightly colored *saput* to tie around our sarongs before entering the temple. He tells us that there will be a shadow play performance by Gedé, Bali's most popular *dalang*.

The temple is not far away. It's just a short walk down the path behind the homestay. I hadn't realized that we are so close to the center of a village. As we enter the temple, the local guys acknowledge us with "*bagus*" and accompany the greeting with thumbs up. Some I recognize from the beach. We're the only Westerners here except for Big Swede, who's already inside.

Anyway, I'm glad the homestay parasites were too stoned to come. The Balinese don't do drugs. Ketut says that the Balinese stay away from anything that can master them—like alcohol or mushrooms. He can't understand why Westerners are always asking for magic mushroom omelets.

"Because they open your mind," I tell him. "I've had plenty psychedelics. No more. I want to experience Bali without getting stoned. Anyway, it's intense enough here already. Who needs it?" Ketut looks confused.

As I climb down the temple stairs, I step on the bottom of my sarong and down it comes. One of the local guys shouts "bagus," and laughs good-naturedly. I grab it and quickly re-tie it.

Twenty or more lithe young women pass us with huge offerings on top of their heads. I am too slow to focus my camera before they move out of the good light. All kinds of stuff is piled 2 or 3 feet into the air: fruit, rice cakes, coconuts, flowers, palm leaves, pork fat—all elaborately carved, stacked and sculpted together. The women exude the most exhilarating smells. Most have hibiscus flowers behind their ears. Some smile at me. Some look shyly away. I am mesmerized—excited by their sensuousness. They are exquisite creatures.

"I'd really like to make love to a Balinese woman," Eddie says as he fixes his eyes on a shapely girl nearby. She laughs in return.

"Who wouldn't?"

One by one, the offerings are unloaded by a priest's wife and placed on high platforms behind three white-clad *pedandas* (priests), who sprinkle holy water on everything. Ketut tells me that later they will take the offerings back home for tomorrow's lunch.

Gedé, the *dalang*, begins an elaborate ritual. He pours holy water, chants some incantations, and adjusts the flame above his head. He washes his hands in the flames, and then rubs holy water into his hair and face. He takes a drink and finally taps on the puppet box with three sharp raps to bring the puppets to life.

He takes the puppets out one by one and arranges them on the appropriate side of the screen. One rather ugly character with disfigured lips and large feet appears.

"He's a bad-looking character."

"No, he's really noble and good. He was just born into a bad family of liars, murderers, and seducers of women."

"Then why doesn't he join the 'good family' if he's so noble," I ask.

"Oh, no, it's his *karma*," Ketut replies. "He must stay in his family. No change. It's his duty. *Mengerti*?"

I get only little snippets of understanding from Ketut. His English and my Indonesian are on an equal par—real bad. I have to fill in the blanks myself, so my understanding of things has to be a work in progress.

The puppeteer is a kind of priest. He must learn the sacred and ancient Kawi language (which most Balinese don't even understand), and he must know which stories to perform for what occasions (births, weddings, funerals, temple ceremonies, etc.). Gedé is the most popular dalang in all of South Bali and may perform 200 nights a year in villages all over the island.

The *wayang kulit* begins. Gedé jabs the handles of various performing, stenciled, leather puppets into a soft, banana palm log at the bottom of the screen. It's fantastic that Gedé, who is relatively young, creates voices so old. He has a tremendously handsome face and large lips, which he contorts with every puppet's voice.

I think I am hallucinating. Sometimes Gedé looks 15 feet tall, other times only a few inches high. Maybe it has something to do with how he projects his power.

Just then Gedé gives a loud shout and begins a moaning, longing chant. With a mallet grasped between his toes, he whacks the puppet box; this signals a four-man ensemble sitting cross-legged behind him to hammer away on *genders* (xylophone-like instruments). The flame of an oil lamp above Gedé's head casts flickering shadows of the delicately carved leather puppets onto the screen.

"Now that's real mastery," I say to Eddie. "If I knew as much about filmmaking..."

Just then Gedé turns around and signals for me to move closer and sit beside him. Who? Me! Gedé's assistant motions to me, and the crowd of men make a small path for me to pass. *Messages.*

I sit down beside Gedé next to the screen! I can feel the

heat of the oil lamp above my head and the hot wind, as he flashes the leathery puppets inches from my face. We are only separated by the thin membrane of the screen from hundreds of people watching a few feet away. What a great privilege.

Gedé channels the voices of the puppets. Closing his eyes, he brings different personalities and human qualities to each as they speak to one another. The puppets are archetypes. I recognize the qualities of bravery and refinement in the prince. And slovenliness in one of the clowns.

One of the prime ministers in the "bad" family has an energetic, wild-eyed look, like Eddie. Next is a philosophical scene. Now the clowns, burping and farting and fighting. The crowd goes crazy with laughter. I wonder whether Eddie likes this or whether this ritual stuff turns him off.

I love this shadow play! There is every type of character: gods, mentors, tricksters, threshold guardians, and holy men. The puppets range from tiny, refined princes and princesses to large, horrific demons.

During the fight scenes, Gedé really shows his stuff. He moves dozens of puppets at once. Armies of monsters attack brave princes; arrows and boulders fly through the air. The power of the gods turns the arrows back; demons scream ghastly death cries. Yes! Gedé deftly places a large leaf-like puppet in the center of the screen. The forces of good prevail. Balance is restored—if only temporarily.

I put my hands together, prayer-like. Bowing slightly to

Gedé, I thank him for the sacred experience, "*Terima kasih, wayang kulit.*"

Unceremoniously, he nods and begins to put the puppets back in their box. My foot's asleep. I limp away. It's not just my foot that is asleep. I've been asleep for months. I've got a lot of learning to do. I want to learn as much about the Balinese way of life as I can. About the shadow play, the stories, the music. Everything. I want to live as they do.

I keep Eddie up all night talking.

"You know, that puppeteer was really great. Do you think he was in a trance to do all those voices?"

"Yes," he agrees, "he certainly was in touch with The Creator."

"The shadow play predates movies by thousands of years. It's got everything, and one guy does all the 'shots,' dialogue, and sound effects. Incredible," I exclaim.

Eddie is not as enthusiastic about the connections between the shadow play and motion pictures as I am.

"It's kind of archaic," he mumbles.

"I disagree completely. This is a living, dynamic art at its best. It's not off in a museum somewhere. It speaks directly to the people."

"Well, Nick, if you want to know the truth, I didn't watch much of it. Over in the corner, these old ladies began dancing like young girls. Now that was exquisite."

"Trance? Do you think?"

"Undoubtedly."

"Eddie, none of my friends even know this stuff exists. And we're living right in the middle of it!! Listen, let's get off this beach and into the culture and really learn something. Become somebody different."

"I'm with you there, buddy."

It's great to share all this with someone and be on the same wavelength. We laugh and talk until dawn.

Chapter 6

LEARNING TO SPEAK

A few days later in Denpasar, I find a student handbook on shadow puppetry. They actually teach shadow puppetry in the university here. The book is written in Indonesian and printed on cheap newsprint. It's almost a comic book. Maybe I can figure it out. Several dozen of the main characters are identified. Let's see. There's *Bima*, *Arjuna*, *Semar*, *Sangut*, *Delum*, *Murdah*. I recognize these characters from Gedé's performance. I also buy an Indonesian dictionary. If I don't learn some more Indonesian, I won't get anywhere.

Eddie's way ahead of me. I guess you have to know lots of languages if you are going to convert the world.

Eddie's genius is apparent. He is already clicking into the Indonesian language much faster than I am. He knows six languages: French, Italian, German, Russian, Hebrew, and Greek.

We sit at a warung which Eddie calls his "language lab." I think he likes it because of the Javanese girl that runs it. She's impressed with him.

It's not long before some old men and boys start gathering around, fascinated by Eddie. I study his technique.

He hears a new word spoken and speaks it back immediately. Sometimes he deliberately changes the sound to see how far he can go before it becomes another word. For example, he'll say the first part of a word, like "ku," and then see how many varieties with meanings he can find... *kuning* (yellow), *kunir* (saffron), *kunjah* (to chew), *kuno* (old-fashioned), *kuntji* (lock), *kuping* (ear), *kupu* (butterfly), *kura* (land tortoise). He may learn six or more words at a time, which then quickly becomes a permanent part of his vocabulary. Then he'll try to make a nonsensical sentence out of the words he's just learned. The kids love these games. He winks at the girl. She winks back.

I have to say one word over and over to myself and then think how to use it and what it means. I give myself a visual image to jog my memory. The Indonesian word for sleep is *"tidur,"* so I visualize a large letter "T" painted onto a door. This seems to work fairly well, but then I have to remember the visualization *and* the sound that accompanies it before I get the word I want. Seems like the long way around.

Eddie is very confident, as the girl serves him another tea.

"The trouble with you is you're afraid to try."

He's right. I might get it wrong. When I was in Hong Kong, I was hanging out with a Chinese rock band. They had a lot of fun teaching me slang words. We went out to a restaurant, and I ordered "a woman's private parts with a raw egg over rice in a bowl."

The waitress freaked, and so did I.

"The people are more forgiving here," says Eddie. "You

can really screw up, even insult them, and they'll blame it on not enough offerings, not you."

I do love Eddie's fearlessness. You'd think being cooped up in a seminary for years you'd lose your edge. With Eddie it's just the opposite. He's ready to try anything.

Me? I feel softened being in Bali. In San Francisco I was assertive. I got it done. I invented midnight movies. At twenty-two, I'd made a film that went to Cannes! I was about to make another film until the draft got me. But here, I don't have a clue. I think it's better to cool out and watch until I've learned the ropes.

Not so for Eddie. He's diving in head first. He's always 'on.' Talking it up with the guys, flirting with the girls, coming up with ideas, excited, ready for action. He loves to be the center of attention, provoke a reaction, and make friends. I leave Eddie at the warung and go off toward the beach.

I walk a few kilometers down the beach, then circle back through the interior. Near Kuta village, I come upon two farmers. One is leading his water buffalo back to the village; the other carries a huge bundle of grass. We meet on a small path. Their faces are clamped tight as walnuts, until I say "*salamat sore*" (good afternoon), and then their faces explode with humor and love.

It takes an enormous amount of energy. The sights, the smells, the sounds. The strangeness of everything. I frequently have to stop, rest, just catch my breath. There are people everywhere. And they are always looking, watching, engaging us. Thousands of eyes upon us.

I head back to the homestay to refresh myself after my adventures.

As I walk in the door, I interrupt Eddie and the warung girl. Eddie has his back to me. The girl is lying on the bed naked. Eddie sits on the side of the bed and talks to her. She doesn't seem to understand what Eddie wants and keeps trying to make love to him. Eddie backs away. I leave them alone and walk back down the beach.

A few hours later I return and say to Eddie, "congratulations."

"Congratulations, what?"

"You slept with her?"

"Well, not exactly...but could have."

"Could have?"

"If I wanted to."

"You didn't want to?"

"No."

Chapter 7

FEVER OF DREAMS

I am reading the *Ramayana*, the great Hindu classic about Rama and Sita. The fever hits me when Rama shoots his magic arrow into the demon's head. My whole body aches. My head is pounding. I can hear my heart pushing blood through my body. *Ke-thump, ke-thump, ke-thump, ke-thump.*

Everything goes fuzzy. I can't hold the book anymore. I only make it to the toilet hole in the ground with Eddie's help. I open my eyes as Eddie wipes my forehead. Sometimes he talks to me softly, but I can't understand him. Other times, there are people I don't know in the room. I try to talk but my throat is dry. I can't hold my eyes open. I drift. Dreams and reality mix.

I am lost in a dark, earthy temple. Corridors stretch out in all directions. Flying a few feet off the ground, I touch the walls to steady myself. They are wet. I leave my handprint in the muddy wall as I pull myself forward floating. Behind me, my handprints turn into ancient texts and illustrated manuscripts thousands of years old.

My feet brush the ground, emitting sparks. I enter a bright courtyard. A large, fleshy man sits eating fruit. I sit in front of him. But as I look more closely, I see that he is filled with holes.

The holes go right through him. Inside there is gold. I look up and see that he's part puppet. He starts singing this wondrous melody in a woman's voice. He stretches out his hand and opens it.

In it is a brick-size chunk of mud. He wipes it clean with his other hand revealing a beautiful silver box. Then all these chorus voices start reverberating. They are a gamelan made up of silvery voices. It's very beautiful, and I want to stay and listen. A single voice becomes clearer and clearer. It's Eddie, and I awake. He puts a glass of tea to my lips and helps me as I drink.

The tea revives me. I lay back down. "Man, I ache everywhere."

Eddie rubs my shoulders, back, arms, and legs.

"That feels great."

I ask what day it is. Eddie tells me I've been delirious for three days. I haven't eaten anything and have been sweating like crazy. He makes me drink some more. It's good.

We talk for a while. I tell him that we need to leave here. We've been on Kuta Beach too long. Maybe the black magic beach made me sick. After all, it is *kelod* here; we're near the demons. Maybe it's the rock and rollers next door. Whatever it is, the vacation is over.

"We have to leave. We're still just tourists. We've hardly scratched the surface. I might as well be back in San Francisco."

"Yeah, or in jail. Or did you forget? Hey, we've got the beach almost to ourselves. The food is cheap. Come on. It's paradise here."

"But it's not Bali. Banana pancakes every morning just ain't it. I'm looking for the real Bali, authentic Bali, not a hippie hotel."

He starts to resist again.

"I'll do it with or without you, Eddie, really I will."

Too tired to argue, I try to sleep. The stuffy night air is like a heavy wool blanket. I sleep without a sarong. There is no breeze. I have a disturbing dream.

I am standing on a beautiful beach. Eddie and I are here for some kind of celebration. Balinese women line the beach dressed in magnificent golden headdresses and transparent sarongs.

The tide comes in and lifts me up. I look down. I'm standing on the water. This is so amazing, I can't believe it. I'm afraid if I move that my feet will break the surface and I'll fall in. Below are large electric eels. I know they are electric because they have Eveready batteries built into their backs.

On the shore, Eddie has erected a bamboo tower. He's just finished folding some palm leafs into a star design, which he is putting at the top of the tower like a Christmas-tree ornament. He begins to climb.

The bamboo tower is rotting before my eyes and cannot possibly support his weight. I am too far away for him to hear me yell. To warn him, I must move but risk falling through the surface of the water onto the electric eels.

In the morning, I feel a little better. Eddie sleeps in. He looks exhausted. He obviously was up all night. When he wakes he won't say what he's been doing. He goes out and doesn't return until it's almost dark.

Night. The *Barong*, the mythical, lionlike creature, will visit our homestay tonight as part of a ritual cleansing. I squat down and wash myself with several buckets of cold water, then put on a clean sarong. A fat lizard darts across the ceiling overhead, stops and stares down at me.

"Hey, Bubba."

The house lizard brings good luck, according to Ketut. I just hope he doesn't fall on me tonight.

I feel much better but am still weak. I rest in the doorway and wait for the Barong. Where did all these people come from? The dusty road behind our losmen is lined with our Balinese neighbors. Big Swede strides up and joins me and Eddie.

A walking gamelan of drums and gongs comes near. The repetitious, syncopated beat becomes louder and louder. It makes you want to move, groove, and trance out.

"I never miss a Barong performance," says Big Swede over the music. "And if it's not a good one, neither will the gods."

"The gods?" shouts Eddie, becoming more and more curious.

"Like anyone else, they won't come unless the entertainment is good."

I look into the street. More people are gathering. The only other foreigner is an intellectual-looking woman in neatly pressed khaki shorts and a shirt. A large amber necklace is around her neck. She writes shorthand in a notebook, concentrating on one of the priests. She pushes her hair from her face.

The gamelan sends out waves and waves of intoxicating repetitions. Eddie looks spaced out. I feel a little light-headed myself.

Suddenly, the creatures rush out. Swede points out the 'good guy,' the *Barong*, a lion-like creature with a magnificent golden coat of glittery, swirling ornaments and a high-arching tail who stomps up clouds of dust. Then *Rangda*, a female monster, rushes from the shadows.

Big Swede, keeping his eyes on the performance, says, "This is the quintessential Balinese ritual where they observe the balance between life and death. Rangda represents death and decay and Barong, the life force. Everything must be kept in balance, that's why there is no winner in this confrontation."

Swede and I step closer to get a better view.

Suddenly Barong, the protector, and Rangda—the destroyer of rice fields, bringer of sickness and death—spring into a life-and-death battle. Gas lanterns cast a golden light across Rangda's long fingernails, saggy breasts, and hairy body.

Surprisingly, Barong is overpowered by Rangda. From the side of the road, the half-naked, fully tranced-out warriors wave kris (magic swords) and attack Rangda.

Swede stumbles and falls somewhere behind me. A dozen men charge repeatedly, but each time Rangda's power turns them back. Someone is going to get killed! The khaki woman is pushed into me. Her notebook bounces off my head. We are caught between the trance warriors and the beasts. Charging, then retreating.

It's not a performance! The ritual play is clearly out of control. They've gone too far. At Rangda's command, the trance dancers fling themselves onto the blades, turning and twisting, trying to kill themselves. The woman grabs my arm and screams, "My god!"

I think I see Eddie rush into the frey.

The warriors' eyes roll back in their heads. Mass hysteria?!! Suicide? The men lean hard into their swords, but their skin is not punctured. Somehow the power of the Barong protects them.

Barong charges again. Rangda is chased away and retreats into the cemetery behind the temple. A gang of children chase after the creatures; Eddie follows in hot pursuit.

As suddenly as it started, it's over. The woman clings to me. We stand on the road dazed, a dozen trance dancers lying around us semiconscious in the dust. It looks like Custer's Last Stand. Should I help? A priest walks among them and sprinkles holy water on the warrior-dancers. Jerkily they open their eyes, find their way out of trance, stand and walk unsteadily away. Swede is nowhere in sight.

The woman slowly releases her grip, her breast brushing my hand.

"I am sorry. I was scared," she apologizes.

"It's okay. You all right?" I ask.

She nods. "I didn't expect this."

I pick up her notebook and hand it to her. She's dazed and confused.

The lanterns are carried off to the family compounds, as the crowd disperses. We leave the dark street and return to my room in the losmen. We are brought some tea.

"I guess balance has been restored," I joke, as I light the oil lamp.

Her name is Anna. She just arrived from Sydney. Her first trip. She's a grad student in anthropology and doing her thesis on rites of passage. Although very young and brave, she's definitely over her head.

"I should go," she says putting down her tea, not knowing that her bemo ride back to the Bali Hai Hotel is long gone.

I explain she has no chance of getting a ride from anyone this late. "The Balinese are afraid of the dark."

"So am I," she says, still shaken from the trance dance. Gradually, the adrenaline wears off and we lay back on the lumpy mattress and talk. The night breeze is cool. The palm fronds rustle above. A gekko snaps at moth, catching it in its jaws.

Anna pulls closer. Before long we are in an embrace and our bodies begin a dance of their own. She surprises me. Her lovemaking betrays her demure appearance. She strains, twists and turns, releasing her deepest feelings.

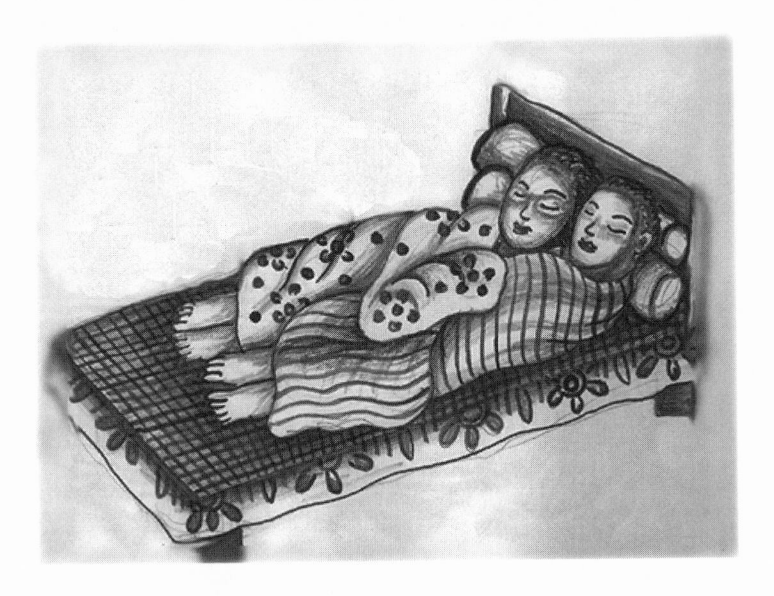

Eddie wakes me up in the middle of the night. He barely notices the naked woman in my bed. He's all excited about something.

"Nick, I followed Rangda and watched. This old guy took off the mask," Eddie says. "He gave it to a priest who hung it in a wooden closet in the temple. It was surrounded by offerings."

Anna wakes up startled. "Who's there?!"

"Just Eddie.

"Come on, Eddie, let us sleep."

"No, listen, Nick," Eddie persists, "when they left I waited for awhile and then snuck into the temple."

I sit up. "You what?"

"I want to go," says Anna afraid, looking around and grabbing her clothes.

"To get a better look at it," Eddie explains. "It had a necklace of entrails. Nick, I put it on. It stank. Then I could feel it breathing! The mask was breathing, and I started breathing with it. I could see into the darkness. Then my blood got hotter and hotter. So I took it off." Eddie is shaking. Shadows from the oil lamp lick the wall.

"Jesus, Eddie, are you nuts?"

"No, listen," he says. "I know where it is. You've got to try it."

"I'm going," says Anna.

I tell Eddie that I have no intention of breaking into their temple.

Anna screams for attention, "I want to go back to the hotel, now!" It takes me a hour to calm her down. She's really losing it. In a strange land, with a strange man, who has a strange friend.

Chapter 8

GUARDIAN ANGEL

In the morning, a wrinkled-khaki Anna joins me for banana pancakes and coffee in the courtyard. She's embarrassed by her intense feelings.

"About my flip out. I just got very frightened. It was dark, then Eddie..."

"It's okay. Could happen to anyone," I say.

"You must think I'm pretty green," she says, shaking her head.

"Think of it as a rite of passage," I joke.

Eddie comes in and joins us. He greedily downs his own pancakes, then mine, then Anna's, which she hasn't touched.

Anom, the manager, stands at the doorway and talks with some older men. They seem to be looking for someone. They peer in at us suspiciously and then leave. Anom comes over. Apparently someone broke into the temple. Do we know who did it? Anna bites her tongue. Eddie feigns innocence.

Now we're really fried.

"Time to go, Eddie," I whisper to Eddie. He agrees. But where?

I find a bemo for Anna that will take her back to the Bali Hai. "Nick, I won't forget you."

"Bali's a small place. See you again."

Back in the room Eddie and I pack our gear. I write a postcard to Adrian as Eddie takes a quick shower.

> *Dear Adrian,*
>
> *We saw the most incredible ritual last night. The Balinese have no problem expressing their dark side.*
>
> *We are just the opposite, aren't we? We repress the shadowy side, don't we? Pretend it doesn't exist. What would happen if we allowed it to fully emerge in our temples and churches? Would America be a less violent society? Would rape, murder, child abuse, and wife battering be nonexistent, as I'm told it is here?..or...*

A familiar smile appears in the door frame.

"Hallow, remember me? I'm Madé Gitah."

"Of course!"

He's our Balinese shadow with features from a Bosch painting: square teeth, cat's eyes, and dark hair that cascades onto his forehead. He unrolls a large painting on the floor in front of me.

Big Swede was wrong about these. These are really fantastic paintings. Much better than Swede's favorites, the crass bright green and orange Penestanen paintings. Gitah's paintings are from Sindu, a village in East Bali, with an entirely different painting style. Inch after inch of canvas is covered in fabulous detail. You can see each leaf in the jungle tapestry painted with remarkable reverence. As if everything mattered to the painter.

"You leave Bali?" he asks.

"No. *Belum.*"

"Kemana?"

"Tidak tau."

"You want come to my village? See more paintings?" he inquires in a childlike voice. His words are answers to our prayers.

"Bingo. You're on," I say. I nudge Eddie and smile, "See, you get what you need in Bali."

Eddie winks and nudges me, "Messages, messages." Madé Gitah draws a map to Sindu village and says, "No problem."

Wrong. Big problem. Eddie and I are in a maze of rice paddy paths. Madé Gitah's map doesn't show the myriad of paths leading in every direction in the rice fields. We walk to the top of a hill where we can see row after row of emerald - green rice terraces covering every conceivable space. It takes my breath away.

"This is wonderful. You know this place is utopia. Let's live here!"

For hundreds of year, the rice terraces have been hand sculpted! It's like that everywhere we've been. You can feel the sacredness of every part of the terraced landscape. I stand in one spot, turning in increments, and take pictures. Taped together, later the photos will show panoramic view of the entire vista.

On both sides are rice fields, and in the distance, a huge volcano releases a string of smoke that snakes its way to the clouds.

"It could blow any minute," says Eddie. "Is that great or what? No one could find us here. Not the draft board..."

"And not your father," I add.

We walk a little further and see a stone shrine dedicated to the rice gods. Beside it is the world's smallest hut. Out pops a small, wiry elder; he squats, squints, and then smiles a toothless grin. With the energy of a small child, he speaks incomprehensibly—in what must be an old Balinese language.

He speaks louder, thinking it will help us understand. (Why does everybody do that?)

This 30-x-30 foot plot of land where we sit must be under the care of the old man. Does everyone here work into their advanced age? This rice field stands out from the surrounding paddies. As miniscule as it is, the paddy is absolutely healthy and pristine. It's more like a spiritual garden. Each plant is perfect. There are no indications of insects chewing on the delicate stalks.

Even Eddie's Indonesian is of no use. The old man never had reason to learn the Indonesian language which was created in 1928. We sit around talking, smiling, and laughing without understanding a word. This doesn't seem to matter as he rambles on, stopping momentarily to spit a stream of red betel nut juice between my toes.

"Imagine growing old in a place like this."

Some other farmers begin to gather—word of strangers travels fast. Broken English meets broken Indonesian. Many eyes are upon us. We are somewhere on the outskirts of Sindu village, lugging our cameras and worldly burdens behind us. Eddie easily engages the young farmers in conversation.

A barrage of personal questions.

"*Dari mana*?" (Where are you from?) a brave boy in a red t-shirt asks.

"San Francisco, di America," Eddie replies.

"*Mengapa disini*?" (why are you here?) someone wonders out loud.

"*Kami suka Bali.*" (We like Bali.) I respond.

"*Dimana tinggal?*" (Where do you stay?) a young man about my age asks. I think his name is Lobo.

"Nowhere... How about Sindu?" I propose. Oh oh, this causes great concern.

They argue among themselves. About our request? This must be serious. No one wants to answer.

Eddie says, "They've got a real problem here. They can't turn us away. We might be gods."

It's a pleasing thought.

Finally some consensus is made, and we are taken into the village to the mud-walled compound of Dewa Sadia, the village leader.

"Yes, yes, yes!" I whisper to Eddie as we walk. I can barely contain myself. This is really happening. We are really going to stay in a village!

Sadia's eyes sparkle in a youthful, moon-shaped face. His smile is his principal feature. He looks our age, but in fact is much older. His English is quite good. He acts as if he's been expecting us.

"Salamat datang. Welcome to Bali! I am glad you come to my village."

What a relief. With a good humored scowl, he orders the gaping youngsters—who don't know what to make of us—to fetch some snacks. In a few minutes, hot coffee and chalk-dry cookies are delivered. Although we are parched, we've learned that it's polite to wait to drink until the host offers the drink three times. That's once, twice, go for it. We lift our glasses on his third sip.

He's warm and sincerely interested in us. We tell him about ourselves.

"We want to live like you, learn from you," I say.

"It's good. I can learn from you. West and East. Rich and poor. I help you. You help me. Everything in Bali like that. Bagus sekali."

Across the compound, I watch Ibu, Sadia's grandmother, instruct a dozen little girls in the family garden how to collect herbs and flowers. Triumphant, they return the herbs to Ibu, who uses a mortar and pestle to crush them into a special powder. One of the nursing mothers sprinkles it on her breasts then draws the infant near.

"The powder's sweet smell keeps the babies very happy!" Sadia says, smiling.

Sorry to break the spell, I stand up. I've got the runs real bad again. Sadia leds me to the *rumah ketjil* (small room) with a hole in the center. Pigs rummage around and sniff at the flimsy door to the bathroom.

When I return, he suggests we leave our gear on the porch and join him for a tour of the village. Dare we? Is it safe?

We walk into the village, down a simple unpaved footpath. The local dogs bark incessantly from the entrances of each compound. It's so loud we can't talk. The noise draws people from their homes and in moments the streets are lined with hundreds of people. Everyone smiles and waves to us goodheartedly. The kids shout, "Hallo, Hallo, Hallo. *Minta wang*." What a welcome.

Sadia points out the family compounds on each side.

"This house; Lobo; this house: Madra, that house: Rani. All painters."

He tells us that his older brother studied with the famous German painter Walter Spies in the 1930's and now teaches the other painters in Sindu. Sadia is now organizing a painting commune. The paintings are sold by Madé Gitah.

Except for Walter Spies, Westerners have only once visited here in the last thirty years, but never stayed.

"Good for you. Good for me," he smiles.

Just then Madé Gitah comes out of one of the compound wearing a new colorful shirt. He shakes my hand vigorously. The hero of the moment, he greets me like a long-lost cousin. The crowd roars. With all this excitement, you'd think they'd declare a village holiday—Madé Gitah Day. I imagine he thinks it will be just a matter of time before we'll buy all his paintings.

Sadia guides us to the main temple with its ornately carved cornices and gateway. Next to it is a huge tree with vines which hang down like the hair of Rangda.

"Wow, look at that. You could live in that tree. What is it?," asks Eddie.

"It's a banyan tree," warns Sadia, "if you fall asleep under it at night when the *leyaks* (witches) are about, you will wake up *gila* (crazy)."

Kids chase each other through the spaghetti-like vines that hang down from the huge tree. Sadia points out the *kulkul,* a carved trunk, hanging high in the tree. A kind of drum. Each village has its own secret rhythmic code that only they know.

"If there is danger..." says Sadia quickly, beating an invisible kulkul with an invisible mallet.

"Ke-thump thump, ke-thump, ke-thump."

Outside the temple, women are pounding rice with posts in troughs.

"Listen," instructs Sadia. "Some people say gamelan started like this."

Behind the temple on a half-concealed path is a deep ravine with a stream at the bottom. Sadia leads the way. We climb over large, ancient, moss-covered stones to get down to the water.

"From an old temple." Sadia pulls off his shirt and sarong and indicates we join him in the water.

"Mandi, mandi."

He covers his privates with his left hand and squats in the water. We do the same.

"Whoa, that's cold," whoops Eddie.

Several dozen kids watch from the bushes, tittering at our ungraceful moves over the slippery stream bed. They can't take their eyes off us.

What a life!

We return to the small bamboo hut that serves as the painting commune's studio during the morning, and as the rest shelter during the hot afternoon. Against the walls and in the rafters are dozens of finished and half-finished paintings of demons, princes, and goddesses. It is already dark. Sadia lights an oil lamp.

"You sleep here. Okay?"

"*Terima kasih.*"

Sadia takes us to the porch where food is being laid out on woven mats. We sit and eat Bali-style with our fingers. The thumb serves as a food pusher. There's rice, root vegetables, tempeh (fried tofu), bean sprouts, and something that might be chicken.

Sadia shows us how to mix into our food the small puddles of *sambal* (hot spices) at the side of the palm-leaf plate. A huge audience gathers to watch. Eddie christens the event *drama makan* (food theater), and the crowd roars. Eddie loves showing off, and being the center of attention.

I drop some rice, they giggle. Eddie tops that by tossing food in his mouth like popcorn. Words ripple out and back, sounds of people repeating what just happened or what was said.

Eddie laughs, "We've entered the theater, but we can't get off the stage."

Sadia suddenly pulls Eddie's left hand away from the food he is about to touch. Eddie's act is interrupted. Everyone laughs. Sadia, and others in the crowd, gesture to Eddie's right hand.

"Right hand for eating. Left hand for..." He makes a wiping gesture. So that's how they do it without toilet paper.

Sadia continues the lecture, "Right hand, give something. Left hand, *tidak bagus* (not good)." Eddie is embarrassed, then sullen.

This new rule makes eating even more difficult. You have to remember to pick something up with the right and then put it down, never transferring food or drink to the left hand. I try to keep the left hand in my lap.

More food falls on my lap than makes it to my mouth. Gotta work on my thumb moves.

The spices burn the hell out of my mouth and make my eyes water. I gulp down a glass of tea, which does nothing for my swollen tongue.

Lobo is also having trouble with his tongue. He can't seem to get it around my name, Nicholas, no matter how many times I pronounce it for him.

"Nipas, Nipas," he sputters, shaking his head. Everyone laughs. "*Nipas*" means "thin" in Indonesian. Everybody thinks this is a real hoot. Nipas is what they call me now.

Everyone is having such a laugh that Eddie gets back into the act. He slowly rolls a cigarette, playing to his audience. "We don't really have any choice," he says, "might as well make the best of it."

It's fun but also very tiring to have so much attention continually heaped upon you.

Sadia wraps a brightly colored saput around my waist. As we follow him up the temple steps and through the split, temple gate, Eddie murmurs, "They're having the ceremony because they think we're gods."

Inside, the entire village is sitting in rows. All heads turn toward us. Eddie bows. Are they awaiting us? No, they are waiting for the solemn pedanda, who is engaged on a raised platform, chanting and blessing the offerings.

One by one, women step up and make their donations. The essence of the food is offered to the gods. (At the end of the ceremony, the food is taken back and consumed. Very practical, these Balinese.) Eventually he gathers up a pitcher of holy water and comes down from the platform. The villagers prepare themselves. I imitate what those beside me do. When he comes by, he breaks into a smile.

"This is it!" I whisper to Eddie, who's ready for the ritual.

I hold a flower blossom between the fingers of one hand in a *mudra position* (a hand posture with religious significance). The other hand is held open. The priest takes my hands and tries to move them. I don't know what he's trying to do, so I pull back.

Lobo, who is sitting beside me, laughs as he pulls at my hands, trying to fix them. Suddenly, I realize that I have them reversed from everyone else. The right hand should be on top.

There are chuckles throughout the crowd. I'm embarrassed. The priest smiles patiently. Once I've got my hands repositioned, I cup them, and he sprinkles holy water inside. He pours, and I drink three times. Then he sprinkles some water on my head. I thank the Balinese gods for the good fortune of being here.

The gamelan begins to play. The musicians are dressed in their finest shirts and sarongs. Their foreheads are adorned with headbands laced with gold thread, and a single golden metallic flower on a wire is tucked in at third-eye level. As they play, these golden flowers bounce in space. Their eyes glaze over. The transcendent music sends us all somewhere else. Is the flower purely decorative or does it focus their concentration in some way?

"Look how they stare into the flower," says Eddie, starting to get into it.

"Remember the book I bought in Hong Kong?" I ask. *The Secret of the Golden Flower*? It's all about meditation. When they focus on the flower I bet they can see Sanghyang Widhi."

"I'll have to try it," says Eddie seriously.

When we return to the hut, we are full of questions. Sadia is delighted to talk with us.

"It is good you come to Bali. Everyone must be happy. You help us. We help you. East and West. West and East. We can do something together."

Sadia enjoys telling us about the spiritual qualities of Balinese life.

"In Bali, it's hard work. Every day must work. Make something better. Must pray to God. Everything come from God. Seed come from God. Put in earth. Then rain. Get Food. All God. *Mengerti*?"

He speaks to us as if we are children.

"Example. Water come from God. Everyone must have water to live. No one can keep water. Water must go to every rice field. No village can keep water, or God angry. Everyone must work together."

Two hours later, we turn in. In minutes, we're back on the porch. Too excited to sleep. It's our first night in a Balinese village. There are fresh offerings on the floor, a stick of incense is still burning.

On the wall of the hut are newspaper and magazine clippings of cars, cosmetic models, Coca-Cola, and motorbikes. Eddie points to them.

"This must stop."

Eddie tears down the clippings, exposing the woven mat walls.

"Look at this wall. It's beautiful. They don't need anything from the West but they think they do!

Eddie rolls a cigarette to calm himself, then he puts on a headband that he borrowed from one of the musicians. He experiments, fixes the golden flower onto it, crosses his eyes on it, and bounces to his own hummed gamelan.

"Hey, this really does create an ecstatic state," he says. "Come on, come here, you try." I try but only get dizzy.

Exhausted, I retire to one of the very small but separate rooms in the back of the hut. Eddie takes the other, only a few feet away, behind the woven bamboo wall. Privacy? What's privacy? I hear Eddie in the next room.

I write a letter by the light of the tiny oil lamp.

> *Dear Sonny,*
>
> *...The Balinese spoil their children. They think babies are reincarnated ancestors, so they treat them like angels. They are always in their mother's arms or being carried by siblings. Their feet aren't allowed to touch the ground for 120 days.There are no unwanted children in Bali. Everyone grows up feeling wanted, in a community that cares about them. This may be Bali's greatest gift. Imagine, a culture where everyone is wanted!...*

I fall asleep while Eddie continues to "trance out" with the golden flower. I sleep like a log and wake refreshed a few hours past sunrise.

Small eyes peer at me through the bamboo wall. I poke my finger through the hole and hear gales of laughter, then the patter of little feet running away.

The painters have already come and gone. Their new work is scattered about, drying on the porch. There are new offerings at the doorway.

We are feeling proud to be in a real Balinese village. Sadia's wife shows me a well across the compound where I can wash.

As I shave, I have the feeling I'm being watched. I look around but there's no one there. It's a funny feeling. When I look into the mirror, I think I see a girl behind me. I turn and there's no one there. Really strange. I tell Eddie.

"Magic, Balinese magic," he laughs. "Maybe some girl wants you."

"Fine with me."

Everyone is already at work in the rice fields. Sadia's wife brings us some cold rice, vegetables, and hot tea. Sadia will be gone all day on some painting business. Eddie is frustrated. He wants to ask Sadia about trance.

"I have some questions, really important questions."

"Let's cool it. Look around here some more," I suggest.

We walk through the village and into the rice fields. There is great laughter. People shout and wave to us.

"Kemana? Kemana?"

"Jalan, jalan."

From as far away as the next ridge and raised rice paddies, they shout and laugh and carry on. Eddie slips on the wet path, and the laughter rises again. We wave and dozens of hands wave back. More heads pop up from the fields that are already high with rice. What a great feeling! Instantly, a thousand people have welcomed us to their home.

We follow the path and wade through two streams which take us out of the village to the south, the other side from where we came in.

We reach the main road and keep walking. The hours pass unnoticed. We enjoy several other villages. Men sit together in the shade along the roadside. Under large baskets are proud roosters being groomed for cockfights.

A bare-breasted woman passes, carrying a large basket on her head.

"You know the early missionaries in Hawaii said the islanders were sinful. Went naked and worshipped idols," Eddie says.

"That's what some people think about this place," I add. "The government wants the women to wear tops and the men to wear trousers."

"Exactly. Don't want your foreign investors to think your country is backward!" he says. "I'm afraid that with the exposure to tourists, the Balinese will feel they are missing something and crave motorbikes, cars, and televisions. The banks will gladly give credit at high interest rates and then, they gotcha!"

We stop and look out over a beautiful vista, rice fields and villages, all the way to the ocean.

"This could all disappear in ten or twenty years. They won't know what hit them. They'll be caught in that vicious circle of working to consume things they don't really need. It's really a shame," says Eddie thoughtfully.

"They'll be too busy earning a living to continue the ceremonies and rituals."

We come to the outskirts of Klungkung. There's a very old stone gate badly in need of repair before a bridge that leads into the town. We cross. A few feet further is a sculptured figure with a magic cloth around its waist and offerings at its feet. Eddie looks back at the bridge.

"Maybe there's a way to slow down tourism."

"What's that?" I ask.

"Let me think about it for a while. I'll tell you later," he says mysteriously. "One way or another, I'm going to do something to help these people."

This talk about the plight of Bali sickens me. Literally. My bloated intestines are gurgling again. I have cramps and am in pain. Eddie says, "evil spirits."

Very funny.

When we reach Klungkung, there is a small hospital. I've got to stop and get something for this dysentery.

We enter a small white building. There is a clerk behind an old desk who stands upon our arrival.

"Good morning, sir."

There is a ward on the right with a row of beds. A forlorn women with disorderly hair comes to the barred window and peers through at me, and begins singing.

"Sir, sir, beautiful sir, beautiful day."

I look away.

The hospital is actually a mental ward, *rumah sakit.* It's director is Dr. Li, a kind but overworked Chinese practitioner. He gives me a bottle of charcoal pills.

Eddie and Dr. Li have their back to the woman, only I can see the dance she begins for me. "Can you see me? Can you see me? Beautiful sir?"

I try to focus on what Dr. Li is saying.

"Bali is lucky, hardly any mental health problems compared to your country. According to a World Health Organization survey, Bali has one of the lowest rates of mental illness in the world. And also, one of the fastest recovery rates."

"Why is that?" I ask.

"The communal society takes care of everybody. And then there are the *balian* village healers. You see, Western science completely overlooks the value of spiritual medicine."

The women distorts her face against the bars and reaches her hands toward me.

"Can you see me? Can you save me, beautiful sir?"

"Of a population of over 2 million, only about forty people require institutionalization."

Eddie laughs, "Trance dancers that never came back?"

"No. Villagers that couldn't handle the stress of modernization. Many from Denpasar and Sanur. Usually we can help them."

"Sir, sir, beautiful sir, help me, save me."

"Don't mind her," says Dr. Li turning around and rubbing the woman's hands, "she'll be fine soon."

The woman continues, "When you sigh, sigh, sigh, say you love me, oh beautiful sir."

We thank Dr. Li for the medicine.

As we leave the hospital, I look back. The barred windows are filled with sorry patients watching us and shouting after us.

"Why didn't you save her?" asks Eddie. "Why don't we save all of Bali?"

We walk through Klungkung. In the middle of town is a small homestay. We stop for a Coke at the warung.

"Darimana tuan?" asks the plump girl at the counter.

"Dari America!" smiles Eddie. "Ada, Coca Cola?."

"Ada!" she grins as she hands him a Coke. I take my dysentery pills.

She's charmed by fast-talking Eddie who uses every Indonesian word he knows, and some he doesn't. I don't follow all of it. As they banter, she leans on the counter. We get a good look down her blouse.

The heat of the late morning is stifling. I can barely move. I have the metabolism of a lizard.

"Time to go, Edward," I say, but he ignores me and keeps flirting. I say, "Come on, Eddie, you'll have plenty of time to find a wife."

"Wife?" says the girl excitedly to Eddie. "You want wife. Okay, no problem, I can be wife, okay?"

We continue to explore the rich, fertile rice fields of East Bali.

It's a beautiful island! I've shot several rolls of black-and-white still film. Although Bali is only about the size of Delaware, more than 2 million people live harmoniously.

"I've had my fill of sightseeing. It's been fun, but now that we've found a village, let's learn all we can from the experience."

Eddie turns his head and smiles. "And begin our film about the women of Bali?" he asks.

"Yes, Eddie, the deeper we get into the village, the better film we will make."

Chapter 9

SINDU BE-IN

Dawn. Back in the Sindu village. Roosters are crowing. Sleeping is over. I awaken in a tiny room, the size of a prison cell, in back of the painting hut. This has been our home since we came to the village a few weeks ago.

I step down from the narrow, shelf-like bed. Two steps away is the curtain to the front porch.

Eddie is in an identical room next to mine. I can hear the painters laughing on the porch, as they find their half-finished canvases and begin mixing their paints. I smell the paint and the rich, fresh coffee.

Small brown eyes peer through the bamboo slits, as I wrap on a sarong and rub my face to erase the pressed pattern left by the bed's bamboo mat. They giggle and run to the front porch to await my royal appearance. It's far too early to be the center of attention. I slap on Eddie's wall so that he'll join me and steal the scene.

Sadia's daughter places a tiny, woven-square offering near the door's opening. It has a few grains of rice, some flower petals doused in holy water, and a stick of incense.

I enjoy the painters; most of them are warm and friendly. A few are aloof and just work silently on their paintings. There's Lobo, Madra, Rani, Suweca, and a dozen others.

Kokoh and Sena, in their late thirties, are technically proficient. They are the teachers. Everyone else is our age or younger. Sadia provides the canvas, paint, and coffee. Salesmen, like Madé Gitah, take the paintings to town in the hope of selling them to tourists. More often than not he is unsuccessful, so hundreds of paintings stack up around the hut, under the bed, and in the bamboo rafters above our heads.

Sadia works on a terrific painting. Inside a large circle are two faces, one is angelic, the other demonic. Outside the circle are animals, snakes, and fire which expresses the man's feelings.

"See, this man is quiet, meditating." Sadia points to the second face.

"But here he has angry face, dangerous thinking." Sadia squints his face up like the man in the painting. Then relaxes it.

"He must meditate for balance. You understand? I make this painting and think about my religion. What must I do to be good man?" explains Sadia.

We're not sure about what we are suppose to do.

"Can we paint?" I ask.

"You want make paintings? It's okay, up to you. But now we don't have so many colors." Sadia picks up a few, almost empty tubes of paint. "We must get money for new paints and canvas," pleads Sadia.

"Where do you get these paints? In Denpasar?" I ask.

"Sometimes. Singapore better, but very expensive. Now we have no money to get paints. We very poor," he laments.

It's true. To the right in the compound is a small house where Sadia and his wife, five children, and his mother live. All together, there are maybe fifteen people living in this small mud compound, not counting us.

Directly across from us is a central pavilion with a single wall—the center for a variety of daytime activities, including sleeping. Beyond that is a tiny kitchen, walls blackened by smoke from cooking, wood, and coconut shells stacked for burning.

Sadia sits down with us. Coffee is served in a thick, glass cup.

Sadia continues, "Before in Bali, we get everything from the earth, from God. I have a chicken you need. It's okay, you take it. Everything belong to God. Why I must keep for myself?"

Eddie nods, very taken with Sadia's philosophy.

"I wish Americans acted like this, but they don't. Maybe the pilgrims did when there was still a barter economy."

"Now we must get more paints. But we have no money. Difficult to go to hotels every day by bemo. We must buy motorbike." Sadia frowns, "Bemo too slow and not go to hotels. Too much walking and carrying paintings.

"Maybe now you think you need one motorbike. But tomorrow you'll have a reason to need two, then three, and then everyone will need one," argues Eddie.

Sadia makes a face. "It's okay. In Bali, we not care about things like tourist people. We no have things. Everyone helps each other in the banjar. Every man must do something."

"In America, young people don't live at home with their parents. Sometimes motorbikes take them far away," I explain.

"Oh, tidak bagus," Sadia scowls.

"And when you go to a new place or a new town, no one knows you. You don't know your neighbor," I continue.

"Not help each other?" Sadia asks.

"No. You worry about yourself. You lock your door."

"We no like that. Everyone knows everyone. Help with somebody else children, help grow rice, help make ceremony. Now we must get money to make offerings for new ceremony. I am very worried," says Sadia.

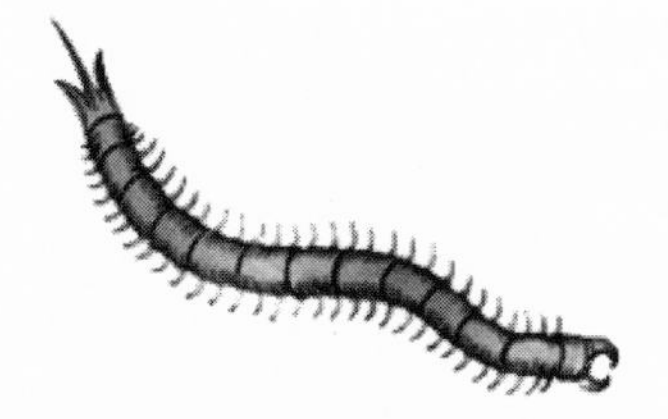

Midday, when it is too hot to paint, the painters lie on the floor all over each other. A head here, a shoulder there, elbows touching, legs drooped over legs—fifteen people, all touching. Like the vines of the banyan tree, everyone is interconnected. If one person shifts slightly, the whole group eventually readjusts.

No one can drift too far away without being gently brought back into the group. There is only belonging here. You cannot be alone. I am touching all of Bali.

Late in the afternoon when it's cooled down, Sadia takes us for a walk along a raised narrow path. The rice paddies may look deserted, but they are a hotbed of activity—a good place to laugh, play, and make love.

"How many paintings does Madé Gitah sell?" asks Eddie.

"This month we make 30 paintings, but only sell two. We have no money," explains Sadia.

Rice paddies surround the entire village. Here and there are clumps of jungle where a village of a thousand people may live. From afar, you'd never know it was here.

"How many rupiah did he get from paintings?"

"Maybe 90,000," says Sadia.

"That's what?" Eddie says, turning to me, "about $45?"

"Not so much. We must buy many things."

"That's only $22 a painting. And they're big paintings. It must cost a lot to make them. You should charge more," I say.

After a few turns and bends, we cross a small stream and continue through another stretch of rice fields. We come to a larger stream with a strong current and walk downstream.

I continue my line of questioning. "So, why don't you charge more for your paintings?"

"We charge good price, best price already. Price not important. I want man to like my painting. No worry so much about price."

We take off our sarongs and squat in the water to bathe Balinese style. The few kids who follow us dive into the water and splash about.

"But if a tourist likes the painting, he will pay much money to get it," I assure him.

Sadia makes an ugly face, not really liking my reasoning.

"If we ask too much money then people not like us."

"See," says Eddie, "they know about fairness. For Westerners, it's 'buyer beware' because someone is always charging as much as they can. Americans are more concerned how they can make money from someone, not how they can make the buyer feel good."

"I think that's true about your country. Money more important than people," says Sadia.

As I float in the water, I think about the tragedy of this.

Just then Eddie splashes me. He calls me "Tom Sawyer;" I call him "Huck Finn." The water runs fast and cool. What a sweet break from the heat. I love it here. This is a great spot.

On the way back, Sadia tells us how he'd like to someday have a big gallery where he can show all the paintings.

A flag approaches us atop a bamboo pole. A pint-sized boy waves and shouts, "Nipas, Nipas," as he commandeers a platoon of ducks in tight formation. I drop to beak-level and shoot off a series of shots as the ducks noisily tumble into the rice paddy water. Sadia tells us that their excrement fertilizes the rice while they eat insects. When the ducks are plump, they are eaten. Total ecology.

Global thinker and environmentalist Bucky Fuller would love it here. I read him extensively when I was in the States. He encourages modern humanity to embrace Nature's principles as the Balinese have done.

Just then we pass the women's bathing hole.

"My God!"

My eyes grow large. The young women don't cover themselves as we pass.

There is no self-consciousness. Several help wash one another. They are exceptionally beautiful. I take several pictures as I walk by. They smile good-naturedly.

"The government has got it backwards," says Eddie. "When you don't wear clothes, you've got nothing to hide."

The main path leading into our village is very quiet. Birds trill among the flowers which bloom high in the treetops.

"When you've got nothing to hide, you tell the truth. When you tell the truth, you can marry a Balinese woman."

We laugh.

A light scent permeates the air as the afternoon light streaks through the trees and bestows a heavenly light onto the cathedral-like forest floor. It is very peaceful until...

Horrid beasts spew forth from the gates of the family compounds on each side of the path and surround us. Damn these creatures! The dirty-haired dogs snap at our rubber sandals. You'd think by now the mutts would be accustomed to us.

Eddie laughs. "The mighty dogs of Bali!"

Sadia picks up some stones and starts pelting the dogs. Balinese don't keep dogs as pets. They are watch dogs and eat garbage or the offerings put out for the demons. You definitely do not want to be reincarnated as a dog in Bali!

We continue down the large path that leads to the center of the village. To our right is a warung that serves biscuits, bananas, peanuts, and other snacks. We sit down and have some tea.

"Here," Eddie hands Sadia a roll of rupiah notes. "For paints and offerings."

Sadia's eyes grow large as he breaks into a smile, "Terima kasih, terima kasih!"

Several men stop talking to stare, as Sadia tucks the money in his sarong. Eyes everywhere.

Chapter 10

TEMPLE OF THE WEST

Morning, and it's drama makan again. There's little food in the compound. We have a few cold vegetables, but even that is a few days' old. Nevertheless, the painters are there entertaining themselves by watching us eat.

"We need a break," I suggest. "Let's go to Sanur and get a hamburger and a Coke."

We catch a bemo to Sanur Beach, which boasts the island's only first-class international hotel. It's not like Kuta Beach, which is cheap and caters to a more rugged class of traveler, but it's still *kelod*, toward the sea, not the mountain.

The bemo stops at the guard gate, and we are waved through. We drive down a winding road past a golf course. Before us across a grassy lawn is the newly constructed Western-style Bali Hai Hotel; the only building that's taller than the coconut trees.

Several drivers laugh and polish their cars while they wait for tourists.

As we enter, we see a security guard shove a young Balinese guy out of the hotel. He throws out a roll of paintings behind him.

"Hey, wait a minute. That's Madé Gitah!"

This doesn't matter to the guard. He elbows Gitah again

as he tries to pick up his paintings. Gitah, obviously very upset, smiles weakly at us and backs away. We go inside to see the Dutch manager.

"Hey, your guard just threw a friend of ours out in the street," Eddie challenges.

"He can't sell his paintings here," the manager replies. "Against our regulations. Our gift shop sells paintings."

"But his village has some of the best paintings in Bali. Why throw him out?"

"It makes the guests uncomfortable to have people like him come so close. Our employees wear uniforms so they know who it's safe to talk to."

"So the Balinese are not allowed in the hotel unless they make the beds or serve the food and wear a uniform?"

"Yes sir, that's correct."

The hotel is a microcosm of the West: restaurants, bars, boutiques, jewelry shops, overpriced Balinese knicknacks, and a go-go lounge. Air-conditioned tour buses with fat, puffy tourists are here today, Bangkok tomorrow. It's a money machine, and someone is getting rich.

By now we're starving.

"Let's get something to eat."

We go into the restaurant and order Cokes and hamburgers. Well, they look like hamburgers and that's what matters. I chomp mine down so fast I don't have a chance to taste it. (Maybe this food will be easier on my system, and my stomach will stop gurgling.)

The piped-in music plays a Muzak version of Dylan's, "Just Like A Woman." We both sing along with the deepest emotion we can muster. We roar with laughter and have a great time. That is until I buy a three-month-old *Time* magazine. The only source of news I've had in months.

The magazine brings me down into a world which I've been trying to escape. There are pictures of Nixon smiling as he gets off a plane, his victory fingers in the air, and Vietnam war pictures. There are advertisements for big cars and the good life.

The guilt overwhelms me. Here we are drinking Cokes and eating burgers in The Temple of the West and listening to sanitized Dylan, and I realize I actually enjoy the familiar.

"Eddie, what the hell are we doing here?" I ask.

We walk out to the beach. We sit on a flat rock and come up with an idea. I write a postcard to Sonny and another to one of my film instructors at the Art Center.

Dear J. J.,

Bali is paradise. I imagine Vietnam was like this before the war. Now there is a new hotel here. My friend and I are afraid Bali is being ruined by tourists.

What do you think of this idea? We want to film the women of Bali except that we'll pretend they are Vietnamese. We shoot them in the rice fields, during the rituals, and with their babies.

These images will sensitize Americans and they will appreciate a rice-based culture. Maybe this will help stop the war.

Can you get it on PBS?

PS. Please destroy this letter after you've read it.

We walk back toward the hotel. In the back is a large swimming pool filled with tourists too afraid to explore the island.

In the safety of a flowered garden there is a restaurant and bar. A couple is surrounded by plates of food. They don't look like tourists. If they aren't tourists, then who are they and where do they live? Eddie goes to find out.

Dr. Robert Richmond, and his wife, Lisa, invite us to sit down with them.

"Too much food. Dig in, fellows."

We decline. He's an anthropologist: bald, bearded, and small. She's a tall blonde with a raggedy mane. Neither are very attractive.

He pulls a piece of chicken from the bone and proudly tell us how he's here "on a Rockefeller Grant" to write a research paper about dance.

"I don't actually dance myself. They pay me to watch." He laughs and takes another bite.

"But how can you write about dance, if you don't dance?" Eddie teases. "Here, write something about this," and does a mock dance.

"See? Words can't adequately describe a transcendent experience."

Dr. Bob laughs and agrees, "Of course, that's why I'm an observer and not a participant."

I tell him that we're staying in a village.

"Did you get a permit?" asks Lisa, dipping a French fry in to the catsup and licking it off.

"Permit? You're saying we need a permit to live in the village?"

"Yes, but they won't give you one. The government wants tourists to stay in the hotels, not in the villages," adds Dr. Richmond, wiping a napkin across his face.

"Of course. You can't make any money from tourists when you can stay in villages for free," grumbles Eddie.

"Just don't get caught. They could deport you," Dr. Bob warns, as he initials the bill.

He stands, ready to leave, as two friends arrive. We are introduced to Pierre and Nicole Devaux, an expensively dressed French couple.

Nicole reaches out for my hand and touches my ring. "Nice, what is it? A carnelian?" she asks.

"Nice necklace," I reply, although she flaunts far too much jewelry in this Third World country.

They join us for a walk on the beach. They are very charming. Pierre works for The World Bank and the central government in Jakarta to develop a business plan for tourism. Nicole is obviously bored. She tries to get my attention, as Pierre rambles on.

"It's a five-year plan which calls for the building of hotels, airstrips, and roads to support 500,000 tourists a year."

Eddie is curious. "That's a lot of people for a small island, isn't it?"

"It's not the size of the island but the number of hotel beds that you can provide. If you fly them in here, you can't have more bums in the planes than you can put in the beds," he laughs.

A jet makes its descent over the ocean, preparing to land in Bali.

"Do you think tourism will benefit Bali economically?"

"Absolutely. Half a million tourists spending a $150 per day for an average of 3 days. If you include everything, that's around $300 million a year!"

"Hmm..." says Eddie.

"I'm not sure much of that will trickle down to the villages. You know, they just threw a friend of ours out of the hotel for trying to sell his paintings," Eddie tells them.

"Eventually the villages will prosper. Right now, the investors in the land and hotel need to see a quick return," says Pierre confidently.

"I bet this land costs a fortune," I say, thinking aloud.

"Actually, it's very cheap," says Pierre, lowering his voice.

"Since not much will grow on it, it isn't worth much to the Balinese," explains Nicole. "How do you American's say, 'dirt cheap'."

Dr. Bob whispers, "You know, for the Balinese this is a black-magic beach. See my house over there?" pointing to bright pink box with a view of the ocean, "It cost less than two grand." He grins proudly. "In a decade it will be worth a hundred grand or more!"

Pierre laughs.

"And it doesn't take much to convince people to sell their land. In fact, the government will help you. They want to see the island developed," continues Dr. Bob.

"What does land sell for?" I inquire.

"Beachfront? Maybe $1,000 or less an acre. In the Balinese economy, the seller becomes a millionaire overnight!"

Nicole turns to Pierre, "It's a barter economy. These people don't use money. So they sell their land and then they have nothing. What can they do with money?"

"Nicole," says Pierre impatiently, "they can buy anything, a car, more land, anything they want."

Nicole shakes her head. "Yeah, maybe, but who sells the car? Foreigners, the government, not the Balinese."

"White man's black magic," I say jokingly.

We continue walking in silence. The beach is exquisitely beautiful, and the hotel gardens highly manicured with blooming frangipani. Bob says that despite the tranquil appearance, things still can go wrong at the Bali Hai. He claims that he was at a hotel dinner for Vice President Agnew. But Agnew was rushed off the island when two of his aides fell violently ill.

I take secret pleasure in knowing that Bali is protecting itself from the evil of the West. Maybe one day the hotel will burn to the ground.

Pierre has to go to a meeting. Nicole follows. We promise to visit the Devauxs the next time we come to the hotel where they stay 'free' as guests of the government.

It's nearly dark as we walk with the Richmonds to their house. They say we can stash our movie camera and gear at their house while we get something to eat at a new restaurant near the hotel. We take only our tape recorder and still cameras, which are like third appendages.

When Dr. Bob sees all our camera gear, he starts asking a lot of questions.

Over dinner, I tell him about the film I made and how it was invited to the Cannes Film Festival and won an award. He is impressed. I explain that I want to make a documentary in Bali. Dr. Bob asks us what we plan to film. Before I can say anything, Eddie goes on a rap about women and balancing energies. He mixes our discussions with Big Swede's rap. The whole thing sounds garbled and unfocused.

Whatever our filming dreams, they are plummeted upon our return. Our 16mm CanonScopic movie camera has been stolen. Only our clothes and raw film stock remain. Lucky for us, we carried our tape recorder and still cameras with us. Eddie is really pissed. Livid.

"It's a message, Eddie," I whisper. "A sign."

"What? We are not supposed to make a film here? No, Dr. Bob is jealous of us and had his servants steal it."

"Unlikely," I say.

We're going to have to take the Richmonds up on their offer to sleep on the floor. That's fine with me but Eddie won't quiet down. He is irritable and judgmental of everything—the hotel, Sanur, the Richmond's lifestyle. Eddie may have studied anthropology at the seminary but he is not trained as an anthropologist. Nevertheless, he feels superior to Dr. Bob.

He says, "If Dr. Bob were really worth his professional salt, he'd be sleeping in a village.

I remind Eddie, "Yeah, and so would we."

I sleep poorly. I dream that one by one all our possessions disappear, no matter how hard Eddie and I try to watch them. I wake before dawn. I can't find my razor.

Exhausted and drained, I start to organize our remaining stuff. Eddie shoves some papers into his pack.

"What have you got there?" I ask.

"Pages from Dr. Bob's books. Here's a cool one from *The Technicians of the Sacred* and another called *Shaking the Pumpkin.* These will please the gods."

"What?!! Are you nuts? You'd better apologize and give them back," I tell him.

Eddie scoffs, "You think he reads these books? He'll never miss them."

Chapter 11

DOGS OF BALI

In the morning we catch a bemo to Denpasar, and putter around on our way back to the village. I pick up batteries for the tape recorder. We never seem to have enough batteries.

We find this great little Fotoshop tucked away off the main road. It's run by Cheng, a Chinese elder who wears a traditional, long-style shirt. His English is excellent. He also speaks French, then German, then Spanish. Eddie and Cheng converse a little bit in each language. Laughing, they hit it off immediately.

I am still fumbling with basic three-word sentences. *"Saya suka nasi."* (I like rice.) I find other ways to communicate. You can always find a way if you are willing to make a fool of yourself gesturing. You have to look into someone's eyes to see if they really understand.

There are four languages being spoken: Indonesian (the new language), the high-caste and low-caste Balinese languages, and Kawi (the ancient religious language, derived from Sanskrit that the gods speak in the shadow play).

For example, "house" in Indonesian is *rumah*, in low Balinese it is *umah* or *balé*, in polite Balinese it is *jeroan*, and in high Balinese it is *geria* or *puri*. That's a lot of words to learn. Even my dreams are starting to be in bad Indonesian.

I give Cheng my few rolls of black-and-white film to process. Cheng's studio has a few props and painted back-drops. Mostly he shoots passport and I.D. photos for the nearby government offices. From under the counter, he pulls out a book with his collection of photos from the 20's and 30's in Bali. Remarkable pictures of a bygone era. Bali has really changed.

Cheng serves us tea and sweets and loans me a flash attachment so I can shoot pictures at night. Cheng is a cool guy. He says we should see Besakih, the mother temple of Bali; it's not to be missed. Several long bemo rides take us into the mountains.

Besakih is located on the slopes of Gunung Agung, which rises dramatically behind the temple. As we start our walk up the steep incline to the temple, we see Big Swede at a warung.

"There you are!" he laughs.

"Where are your girlfriends?" ponders Eddie.

"Back in Sanur resting. Bali is freaking them out. Not everybody thinks it's paradise."

"Well, I do," says Eddie.

"Staying in Sindu are you?" says Swede.

"How'd you know that!"

"Everybody knows everything in Bali," he grins. "I live in Iseh, only a few kilometers away. My adopted father told me two guys were wandering around the rice fields. I figured it was you."

"What we do is none of your business," barks Eddie. "Let's go, Nick."

"Before you go," says Big Swede, "don't you want your mail?"

Big Swede hands over two pieces of mail. Eddie is furious.

"I suppose in Sweden you've never heard of 'the right of privacy'?

"Sorry, I was in town earlier and..."

"Forget about playing postman, okay?"

"But Eddie," I interrupt.

"Nick, you want to hang out with him, fine. I've got something I have to do. I'll meet you at the losmen in Klungkung," he grumbles, as he storms off.

Swede yells after him. "There's a ceremony in Sindu in two days. The village boys wouldn't want you to miss it." Eddie keeps walking.

Swede and I walk around Besakih temple, one of the most sacred spots in Bali. I'm sorry Eddie missed it. What's he up to? Perhaps he wants to see his warung girlfriend.

"What's his problem?" asks Swede.

"You have women. Been in Bali a long time and he's troubled about how tourism will destroy Bali," I reply.

"People have been saying that for decades. Can't happen," says Swede confidently. "Their spiritual power is too great."

Seems Swede is without money again. I buy him a glass of arak. In return, he tells me about another sacred spot.

"Why's it considered sacred?" I ask.

"You'll see."

We are tightly packed in the back of a truck with about twenty priests. The group laughs with every bump in the road which tosses us to and fro. After a while we stop in the middle of nowhere. Everyone gets out and walks less than a kilometer to a small village on the side of a great ravine.

"What's so special about this place?"

"One day, for no apparent reason, thousands upon thousands of white herons arrived in Petulu village," says Swede.

"What do the villagers make of it?" I ask.

"A sign of good fortune. The herons are the spirit bodies of divas, they take flight at dawn and return faithfully each evening."

Just then the sky fills with thousands of white shapes, which circle and curl before landing in the trees surrounding the rice fields.

It's beautiful here. I sit down under a tree to read my mail: a letter from my mother, another from Adrian. Sonny still hasn't written. There is a clipping from *The New Yorker* on the rise of avant-garde filmmaking. The last page of the article is missing.

Dearest Nicholas,

... We are glad to hear from you at last. When your postcard arrived this morning, I read it over and over. Your father and I are glad you are well and happy. What do you eat? Be careful. There are many diseases.... Are the natives very primitive?... Why would you want to stay in a village if there is a hotel nearby?

... How long do you plan to be away? We thought maybe you'd think things over and come home for Christmas. Your grandmother is very sick. Sooner or later you're going to have to work things out.

Your brother has been pouring concrete all summer and would like to see you....

I will go to the box to mail this and then to the club. I have a golf game with Betty, Sissy, and Marilyn. My game has been off all summer but I love it so....

Love, Mother

It's clear she has no idea of what life is like in Bali. And come home? She can't be serious.

The next letter is exciting and depressing at the same time.

Dear Nick,

I hope paradise is treating you well and that you're happy because things are going great here. We're still showing Midnight Movies and getting tons of free publicity. Now there's Midnight Movies everywhere: New York, LA. We still have full houses every weekend. I am showing the freakiest films! Making tons of money which I've been lavishing on a new studio and gear.

Congratulations! "Various Incarnations of a Tibetan Seamstress" won "Best Young Director" at Cannes. Since "Easy Rider" is a hit, the studios are looking for new blood. Can you believe it, I was offered $50,000 to write a script!

They all want to meet you. What should I tell them? It's a shame you can't take advantage of your fame. Since they can't meet you they want you even more!

Wish you were here and we were making our film together.

Love ya,
Adrian

I'm glad for Adrian but more than a tad jealous. I can't deny that in many ways I wish I could be part of it.

Some herons fly from tree to tree. Swede comes up. It will be dark soon. He says we can get a ride with the priests to Sindu. I decline, “No, I’m going in the other direction. I promised I’d meet Eddie.”

I meander back on the road to Klungkung. I’ll hoof it until a bemo comes along. It’s not so bad, it’s all downhill.

It seems strange to be without Eddie. We’ve hardly had a break from each other since we met. We’ve both been making many compromises: when to eat, where to go, what to do, where to stay. Now it feels good to be alone and think my own thoughts uninterrupted.

Damn! It is still many kilometers to Klungkung and getting dark. All the bemos have stopped running. The Balinese don’t travel at night—that’s when the *leyaks* (witches) come out. Terrific. Now it doesn’t feel so good to be alone.

I walk through a quiet village. All of a sudden, every dog in the place surrounds me and barks like mad. Not this again. I bend over to pick up a rock. They move back slightly and bark even louder. I pretend I'm going to throw it so I can walk a few feet, but they don't move. I feel the Cheng's flash in my bag and pull it out, turning it on. When it's fully charged, I flash the unit at the barking beasts. They scatter in every direction and keep a great distance.

Just then, it starts raining really hard. I rush to the side of the road and pull a giant palm leaf from the jungle, and hold it over me—a Bali umbrella. I'm rather proud of myself for remembering what the Balinese would do. It's still pretty creepy alone at night.

I feel better a little later when I join up with some Balinese farmers along the road. Leyaks can't devour all of us, can they? We walk and talk for a few kilometers. One by one, the men turn off onto paths to their villages. I'm alone again and it's very dark. I buckle down and brave it out. I've always felt charmed and protected. Besides, I don't believe in leyaks.

The clouds are so low they hide the stars. There is little electricity on the island and no street lights. I have to feel the gravel beneath my feet to stay on the road. Overhead is some strange movement and light.

As I get closer, I see a lantern held by a farmer as he catches eels in a flooded rice field. He stoops, holding the lantern below him near the water. His shadow is thrown on the clouds above. It is eerie. My wet clothes cling to me. Spooky shadows play overhead. I don't like this one bit.

The gods turn the tropical showerhead up to torrent strength, forcing me to consider shelter. On my right is a deserted pavilion, where cremation towers are being built. A river is being dumped on my head. I can barely see. I imagine leyaks lurking everywhere. Every horror movie I ever saw as a kid comes to mind.

It's absolutely pouring. I walk faster. I'd rather drown than see a leyak. I say a few prayers to the local gods. I come to the outskirts of Klungkung. Finally! It continues to storm. I can only see a few feet in front of me as lightning strikes. I look for a landmark. Here is the sculptured figure with a magic cloth around its waist, but where is the old gate?

As I get closer, I see that the old stone gate has fallen on the bridge and blocked the road. What happenned here! There is debris piled everywhere. It's going to take days to clear all this away. It's pouring as I make my way to the rocks. I don't have a clue which way to go, there's so much debris.

Lightning flashes. I turn and look behind me. There, illuminated is a young girl holding a palm leaf over her head and standing completely still.

"Jesus, you scared me!" I shout.

Lightning strikes again and again, lighting up the bridge and debris. She points to the left and starts to join me. I nod and climb through the debris while I can still see.

What's she doing out in this storm in the middle of the night? She is just a little girl, right? Right!? Maybe seven or eight years old? I spin back around. Where did she go? She was just here! I did see her? Of course, I did. I whisper to the Gods. A leyak?!! Ohh, just let me get to the losmen. I promise I won't walk again after dark, ever! I limp into the Klungkung losmen after midnight.

In a room I find Eddie naked, sitting in meditation before a small statue of Jesus. The surrounding candles throw flickering light across his face. The coconut bowls that he's been carrying from Kuta Beach are half-filled with water and flower petals. Before him is our stolen camera—damaged beyond repair.

Eddie opens his eyes.

"It's becoming clear to me," he says quietly.

"What's becoming clear?"

"That we're the ones to save Bali, to protect them from their future."

"We can't do anything about the tourists."

"I already have," he says strangely, as the candles are reflected in his eyes.

"What do you mean?"

"They won't be able to desecrate the ceremony in Sindu."

"And why not?"

"Didn't you see the bridge?"

"Bridge? What bridge? Ohh, you didn't...?"

"Ha! Let the tour buses get past that!"

A lizard scurries across the ceiling almost slipping.

"I'm coming into my power, Nick," he says, holding up the camera, "Look! That's why I had to come back here. I had a premonition that I could find the camera if I followed my instincts. Three young Javanese guys must be in cahoots with the bemo drivers who tell them where tourists stay. When they left their house, I broke in. The camera was already damaged. They probably kept it because they think it's powerful. I peed on their stolen clothes and suitcases. I've got the power now!"

"It's amazing."

"It is amazing, I never knew I could do something like that!" he says, putting on a sarong.

But the gate crumbling on the bridge? Could he really have pushed it over? No. It must have just fallen and he's taking credit for it. But finding the camera? And peeing on the stolen stuff?

"What are you smoking, Eddie?"

"In the morning, we'll return to the village. Maybe Sadia can help me with the power," declares Eddie.

I try to fall asleep. I think about Besakih temple with Gunung Agung, the great volcano in the distance.

I am not asleep long before my own personal volcano erupts in my stomach with aches and bloating. Then full-blown dysentery sends me out into the night. Exhausted, I lay back down on the bed to sleep.

Just as I recover from the chills and am fading again into sleep, something runs beside me. Something is breathing, almost whispering, in my ear. Then a crunching sound. I open my eyes and prop myself up. I can barely make out the silhouettes... rats?

At first there's just three or four, but as I begin to count them, there are more and more! I am too weak to move. Hundreds, could there be hundreds? I can't believe my eyes. They come in through the door, pass me, and leave through the back of the hut. The Rodent Expressway. I call to Eddie, but he doesn't wake up. The room swells with the smell from their hot, panting little breaths. Tails, like equatorial night crawlers, drag behind them. I close my eyes, hoping this demonic nightmare will end.

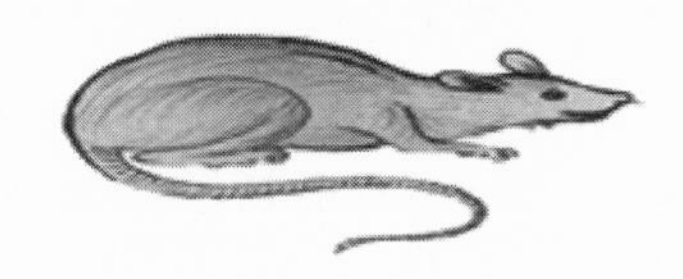

Village. Dawn. I shave and brush my teeth. This is only time I am ever alone. Well, not exactly.

It's happened many times now. I am shaving and have this feeling I am being watched. I adjust my mirror, and there she is...staring, uninhibitedly. When I turned to look, she is gone and there are only pigs foraging through the compost heap. She's only in the mirror!

Today I see her clearly. She is splendor. Perfectly composed and groomed, as if she's going to a temple ceremony. Elegantly arched eyebrows, proud cheekbones, ample lips. Bronze skin resembling highly polished gamelan keys. If I look only in the mirror, she stands watching. She is about to speak but doesn't. Am I her amusement?

My mystery girl isn't the only one I entertain. The painters love watching me. I'm their Las Vegas. All I need to do is eat, or sit cross-legged, or tie my sarong, or bathe, or pee, and I have a captive audience.

It is late afternoon. Eddie and I follow Sadia for our daily *mandi* (bath). Another route this time. We go beyond the main temple, down a path into a very deep ravine. We stop by a small stream. It is very quiet. We squat in a small pool among the ruins of an old temple. Giant trees and ferns shoot up a hundred feet.

The water is cold and feels good. A small waterfall drops from above. Sadia sits under it, letting it hit him in the

mouth. He sings into the water with a raspy, cackling voice—the sound of the monkey. Eddie tries. Sadia says *dalangs* train their voices by singing into waterfalls. It strengthens their voices and shakti. Sadia teaches us a very beautiful song. We try it until we are hoarse.

When we return to the hut, there is a crowd of people. Madé Gitah has brought an Australian to the village. He calls him *kawan* (friend). He has come to collect art. Sadia pulls down the paintings from the rafters of our hut. (Great! Get rid of some of those eyes and teeth paintings!) Some are good, others bad. A few are magnificent treasures by Kokoh, Lobo, Rani, or Sena. Others are by kids. He rolls these up and stuffs them into a beautiful five-foot tubular basket that Sadia's sister made. (The women of the village specialize in basket making.)

I'm not sure about this guy; there's something about him I don't like. Sadia is very trusting. The Aussie is organizing a big painting exhibition in Sydney. When he sells these, he'll send money to the village. Sadia is so trusting. He gets no money for dozens of paintings. He takes the Aussie's word.

Late night. Eddie and I venture out into the village alone. I mount Cheng's strobe attachment on the Leica. We're going to photograph the "Dogs of Bali."

We only get a few yards before the monsters charge. I'm ready. I aim the camera in the direction of the sound, and fire away. The strobe temporarily blinds them, and they race back to the safety of their master's compounds. By the time the strobe has recharged, we are surrounded again. Another flash and we can walk a few more yards. The incessant barking and strange flashes bring entire sleepy-eyed families out of their huts, Sadia among them.

Sheepishly, we return with him to our compound.

Eddie and Sadia sit down. I go into my room. My cotton jacket hangs on a peg and is covered with dozens of immense mosquitoes waiting for their feast, me. I slay as many as I can. The more I kill, the more of me will be left in the morning.

I lean against the matted wall and light the oil lamp, then begin a letter to Sonny. On the other side of the wall, Eddie tries to enroll Sadia in his plan.

"Tourists treat people badly," Eddie says very quietly. "Money, everything is about money. Soon, Bali people will be like this. You understand?"

"Yahh," says Sadia.

"I don't want this. You don't want this. Help me learn Balinese magic so I can stop them."

"You want to study to be *balian*?"

"Do they practice magic?"

"Some do. You must study the lontars, read Bali language," says Sadia.

"No, no, no. I don't have time. I need a magic teacher now to help me stop tourists from coming here," says Eddie impatiently.

"But we need tourists. We must sell paintings to get money."

Eddie only gets more and more frustrated. Sadia leaves the hut confused.

I write long letters home by the light from the oil lamp. Writing gives me a way of examining my own disoriented thoughts.

Dear Adrian,

Your news is great. I'm happy for you. As great as it would be, I can't come back. It wouldn't take the army long to find me. (Are they still looking for me?)

Why not come here? You could write a movie in Bali.

I'm still hanging out with my old friend, the run-away theologian! He's a fascinating guy. We're living in a village. Everyone's an artist. Can you believe it?

We're going to make a film here about Balinese women.

A faint buzz gets louder and louder. A small plane? Suddenly a fuzzy bee—the size of my fist—flies past my head, and out an opening in the roof. At precisely the same time every night, it flies through on its way to a gigantic, nocturnal flower. I name it "Big Buzz." Once you name something, it becomes much less frightening. It is as if you know what it is, even though you don't.

I write another letter.

Dear Sonny,

I wish you'd write. I don't know that anyone else besides Eddie who can understand what we're going through. I have strange, powerful dreams. And waking reality is intense and often surreal. These people look deeply into you. There's been many times where I've understood things telepathically.

The draft and leaving really were a good thing after all. I didn't realize that I needed to be alone and work things out.

What's important here is how you treat your family and friends. And whether you devote yourself to helping the village and honoring the gods.

Eddie, the guy I'm traveling with, wants to fight tourism that's threatening Bali's culture. I want to find another way to give back. These wonderful people have done so much for me....

Love, Nick

PS. Please destroy this letter once you've read it.

Mosquitoes cluster around the end of the pen. When I stop writing, they bite me. It's as if they want to swim in the energy coming off the tailwind of the pen.

I gaze into the oil lamp. Mesmerized by the flame's kindly, soothing lure, I ease into sleep.

Chapter 12

TRANCE DANCE

"We're prisoners here," Eddie says.

"Not exactly," I counter. "We just don't go out very often."

"Prisoners," says Eddie, "Sadia's prisoners."

It's time that we get our own house. It's not that we mind sharing the morning with the painters, or our meals with every spectator within 3 kilometers. We don't want to be ungrateful, but maybe we've stayed with Sadia too long. Maybe he'd like his hut back.

"Okay, why not?" Sadia smiles. "You want? We build new house?"

It sounds great. Especially the deal. We buy the materials and we'll own the house. He'll own the land. If we ever leave Bali, the village will keep the house for us and use it. It will cost a few hundred dollars. Special craftsmen will build it. We agree.

Sadia gives us our choice of several extraordinary locations. One is near a small stream.

"You can live here," he says, "and listen to the water." We walk a short distance. "Or," he says, "you can live under these palm trees." There's also a site a few hundred feet from his family compound, not far from the women's bathing hole. We choose this last site.

A few hours later, a priest comes to the house. He spends several hours consulting with Sadia over the Balinese calendar to determine the best day to build. Things are happening very fast. Had Sadia already planned to build a house or is he just being spontaneous?

"Reality and events are somehow linked to our mental images," I say, thinking aloud.

"It's more than that," Eddie says. "If we *think* something, that starts it *actually* happening. The Balinese feel our thought waves and act on it."

We give Sadia all of our *rupiah* that we changed when we were in Denpasar. He needs it for the special ceremony that will take place in the temple tonight. A group of *Sanghyang* dancers from North Bali have been invited for a trance ceremony.

We visit the temple in the afternoon, already dressed in our finest. There are more than 20,000 temples on the island! The decorations and preparations are well on their way. The priests have begun sanctifying the temple to insure success.

By evening, the gamelan is set up in a separate pavilion. I sit near them and talk with Sadia.

"The gods must consent to enter the dancer," says Sadia. "If they do, much success for your house and Sindu."

It is a warm comfortable night. I smell the frangipani. The gamelan beats out a steady rhythm. One player keeps time on an overturned bronze bowl. Lobo and Rani are the drummers.

There's a "female" drum and a "male" drum on which they play interlocking parts. Other musicians also play interlocking parts on xylophone like genders, creating a quicksilver melody. I can hear the patterns as they unfold, altering subtly and then repeating.

I recognize many of the villagers now, most of whom kneel on the ground. Offerings are spread everywhere.

Two groups of tourists akwardly enter the temple, their cameras dangling from their neck. One women inappropriately wears shorts. Eddie is steaming.

"How'd they get here? " he says irate.

Two young Balinese girls are dressed in golden dresses which sparkle brightly, illuminated by gas lanterns. Everything else is dark-brown shadows.

The priest takes two dolls out of a basket. They are tied on a string between two sticks. He hands the sticks to the two boys who sit on either side of him. They start pulling on the sticks, which makes the dolls bounce up and down to the gamelan. A row of women chant behind the priest. The rhythm picks up. The dolls dance more and more. Occasionally they fall limp but the boys quickly get them dancing again.

The young dancers come forward and kneel over the dolls. They seem to get themselves in sync with them.

Eddie who shouts over the din, "The dolls. That's how they do the entrancement. I'll have to get some. Look!"

The music from the gamelan, the dancers, the dolls, the boys, the priest, and the chanting women build the energy until it's almost palpable. Another priest brings the girls' headdresses. The music becomes even faster and wilder and the chant gets louder. My head begins to swim.

The girls dance in wide circles over the dolls, leaning forward then back, winding around to the ground, dancing, swaying, winding their arms in loops and circles.

Two men walk up to them and kneel, and the girls leap onto their shoulders and balance! They do so without even holding the men's hands. When they land, the men shoot up and the girls rise into the air—still keeping their balance. They continue to dance in this winding, circling fashion. Swaying in larger and larger circles, backwards and forwards.

The men bring the girls to the ground before a pathway of coals. The girls walk over the fire and cinders, dancing, scattering sparks and red-hot coals, completely unaffected by the heat. The tourists shoot off flashbulbs, which breaks my concentration momentarily.

"Hey!" yells Eddie.

The chanting ends and the girls take off their headdresses and wake up.

"I could do that," Eddie says covetously.

Sadia is content. The dance is successful. The gods arrived. It's a thrill for him to see us so agog.

"It's the gamelan, isn't it?" I implore. "The gamelan opens up new pathways in the mind."

I beg Sadia. "Can someone teach me to play?" This must be a serious request, given the expression that spreads across Sadia's face.

"That," he says, "must be okay by the *bale banjar.*" He says he'll ask the village council, which makes all the important decisions by consensus.

"Hey!" says Eddie, "what about me?"

Sadia says, "You want to play gamelan too?"

"No, you know what I want," he says, as he watches the tourists leave the temple. "To learn magic. To go into trance. To stop these tourists." Sadia is uneasy.

"When they are in trance," Eddie inquires, "they can think like gods or spirits?"

"Ya. Same. No difference."

"Many people know how to go into trance?"

"Maybe twenty people in Sindhu go into trance."

"How do they do it?" Eddie asks.

"I don't know," the village leader says.

"But you've seen it all your life," Eddie says, disbelieving and annoyed with Sadia.

"Yes, many times in Bali people do that," Sadia replies.

"Never happen to me. I don't know. The gods pick them."

"The gods pick them?" Eddie asks.

"Of course," Sadia says in a matter-of-fact tone.

"Then they might pick me?"

"You are from America. Americans don't go into trance."

"Some do. Holy Rollers do."

"I don't know about that."

"When they are in trance, what do they do?"

"They talk to us with God's voice. We listen. We are happy they come."

"Trance mostly happens when people dance?"

"Sometimes dance, sometimes music, sometimes with mask. Many times."

"I want to learn to dance! I'll dance, then trance."

"Oh, you cannot."

"Why's that?"

"You must learn to play gamelan first."

Eddie won't leave it alone. He carries on about trance dancing half the night, calling to me with his thoughts from the other room.

"Nick, listen, listen, if I can go into trance, then the ancestors will tell me how to save Bali. What do you think?"

"I think you're pushing it, Eddie. Now go to sleep."

The next day I ask Sadia if there is any word from the *banjar* on my learning gamelan.

He says, "*Belum, nanti.*" (Not yet, maybe later.)

"Do you have a *tingklik*," I ask, "a bamboo xylophone?"

Sadia says, "No problem." He calls to one of his sons, who quickly collects bamboo. Another cuts it to size, tuning it. A third assembles the bamboo tubes together over a frame. In no time at all, voilà… a tingklik!

I play on it for hours. Eddie is right. Once you put in your "order," it won't be long before you get it. Bali is like that.

That afternoon, a surprise. Lobo brings a single *gangsa* (xylophone instrument) from the temple to the porch of our hut. Lobo is fast becoming a good friend. Full of fun and laughs, with eyes that look in different directions. An audience of painters assembles to watch my first lesson.

Lobo is a most patient teacher. He's my exact age, twenty-three. Proudly, he presents me with my own *panggul* (mallet) that he has carved and signed. He hammers out short patterns and then nods for me to repeat them—endlessly. Like a game of musical concentration, the simple patterns stack up, forming long strings of rhythmic melody. The right hand holds the panggul and strikes the bronze keys—one at a time.

The left hand dampens the key just struck by pinching it between two fingers to mute it from ringing too long. This dampening technique allows other players to fill in the spaces with their strokes, creating rapid, interlocking patterns—a waterfall of celestial notes.

Lobo and my audience are impressed by how quickly I learn to play. I don't tell them that I've played drums since grade school. I don't want to ruin the illusion that I am "*pandai*" (clever) and learn quickly. As soon as I master a short section, Lobo adds another. Eventually the piece expands to the limits of my memory.

Now other musicians want to show me their stuff. Each has a flashy way of striking the keys. A flick of the wrist, a spin of the mallet, a bob of the head, a wink of the eye. They love performing. I mimic their flashy movements. They roar. It is easy to communicate through the music lessons. Sadia's wife, Cana, brings out coffee and kreteks. The group takes five.

Eddie leaps to his feet. "If I learn to play, then I can learn to dance, yes?" Sadia nods.

As he steps over the instrument, one of his feet touches the keys. Sadia and Lobo let out a gasp. Lobo looks to Sadia, who makes a face like he's eaten a sour bug.

"Tidak bagus, you must never do that," Sadia scolds. "Feet are low. This is a sacred instrument. Never step over it."

Eddie gets off to a bad start. First he has trouble with "dampening" the keys. Then after seven or eight notes, he can't remember even the simplest pattern. This is strange, because Eddie is an excellent pianist. Too much pressure, I guess. He attacks the keys as though he's got it together. Great attitude. Lousy technique. He holds in his frustration.

Eddie tries again and again to play. But he's shaken by inner criticism and can't concentrate.

Sadia laughs, "You have monkey mind." This irritates Eddie even more. He bungles, striking two keys at the same time. They ring out in dissonance. The painters laugh. The harder he tries, the worse it gets.

I tell him, "Hey, come on, just relax."

He says, "I can do this when I want to."

A rare appearance from the mysterious Ota, who watches Eddie's practice from the sidelines. He doesn't hang out with the other painters, in fact, he doesn't hang out with anybody. He's a little odd. I think he makes masks. Through his smudged tortoise-shell glasses he catches Eddie's eyes, then, walking with a cane, siddles over to talk to him. Eddie is flattered.

"I'm going over to Ota's house," Eddie whispers so that Sadia doesn't hear.

"He'll teach me to dance without me having to learn the music."

Later at night when everyone has gone to bed, Eddie does little made-up dances and pretends to go into a trance. He's really obsessed by this desire.

He says, "I am Sanghyang Widhi. I've come to purify Bali and rid it of all its tourists."

And then he pretends to come out of trance and asks me what he'd said. It's funny at first and we laugh. I encourage him. But he doesn't know when to end the joke.

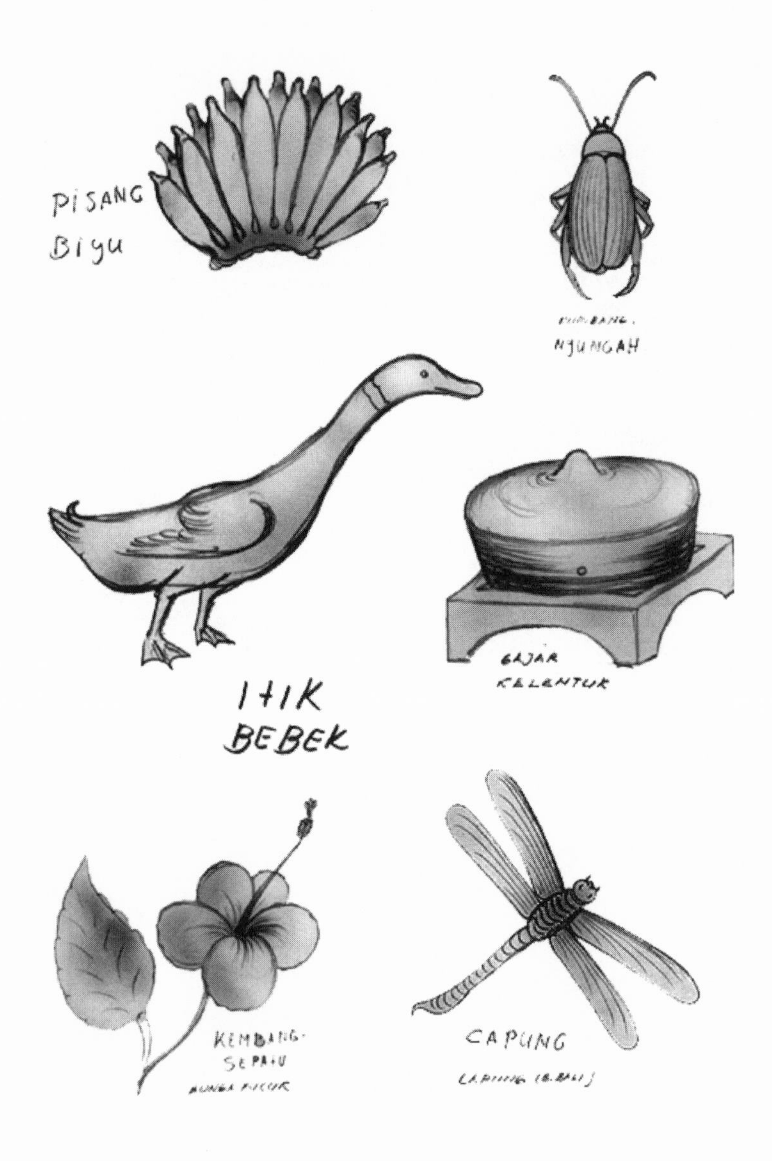
PISANG
Biyu
NJUNGAH
ITIK
BEBEK
GAJAR
KELENTUR
KEMBANG-
SEPATU
CAPUNG

Chapter 13

LETTERS

Sadia's compound is on the outskirts of the village. His sons follow us as we walk out of the village, across a large stream, up a hill, through a smaller stream, past barking dogs, onto a curve in an asphalt road near Sidakaria village. A small shop sells plastic pans, soap, kreteks. We wait for a bemo to take us to Klungkung, then later we'll catch a bus to Denpasar. We see a bemo and flag it down.

When it pulls up in front of us, it is already stuffed with farmers with their machetes, women with fruit-filled baskets, live chickens, several pigs, and lots of children. I think they'll never get us on, yet somehow they do. We grab our sarongs so they don't fall down, and we climb into the tiny compartment—wall-to-wall humanity. No one seems to mind. It's just how it is. A beautiful girl of about eighteen presses next to me. She sits very erect until the bemo hits a pothole and we are thrown together. Her breasts strain under an electric pink bra that's far too small. I can feel the heat from her body. I breathe in her coconut scent. Jeez!

An old woman smiles, showing a single tooth. The small boy clings to her lap, terrified by my hairy legs. The girl glances down and turns away. (The Balinese have little facial or body hair. Only demons are hairy. Do I have to shave my legs to get a date?)

And smell-o-rama! In Bali it's as if my senses have just been turned on for the first time. The sounds, the sights, the smells. The bemo spews fumes into the back, which mix with the smell of humanity. It's a miracle we are not asphyxiated.

The closer we get to Denpasar, the more traffic. Gradually we slow down to a grind. We cannot pass other cars because there are no shoulders on the road. There's just barely enough room for oncoming traffic to pass. The drivers that misjudge the distance end up in one of the channels of open sewage at the side of the road. I'm glad I'm not driving. The road becomes progressively lined with shops and *warungs.* We arrive at Denpasar's bustling bus stop.

The commercial part of Denpasar is about a dozen square blocks, including a large outdoor market, many small shops, restaurants, souvenir stands, banks, small hotels, and government offices. In the center of town is a large playing field surrounded by a museum, the post office, and a hotel.

Our first stop is the Bank Negara Indonesia 1946. I take the snakeskin pouch from around my neck. Seiji, one of my best friends, made it for me. He sewed a *vajra* symbol inside for protection. We change some of the traveler's checks then go to the post office, where letters await us in Poste Restante.

The clerk hands Eddie about three dozen letters which he goes through, looking for our names. Several are for us. He sees one to Big Swede and pulls it out.

"What are you doing?" I ask.

"Playing postman. I hope I don't lose it on the way," he smiles.

"Come on, Eddie, are you still bugged about that? He was only trying to do us a favor. Put the letter back."

He does.

"Can I help it if I don't like that guy?" he says.

But who are these other foreigners? What are they doing here? We buy stamps and send our letters and exposed film back to the States for processing. We make sure that the clerk hand-cancels the stamps because otherwise some enterprising clerks will peel off the unused stamps and resell them, making more than a day's wages.

We visit the warung in front of the post office, one of our usual stops when we come into town. I read my letters while I eat toast, drink tea, and smoke a sweet kretek.

I get a downer from J. J. who tells me PBS is not interested in a film about Bali *pretending* to be Vietnam. (He's jealous of our adventure.)

Adrian sends a stack of film reviews about our "Various Incarnations of a Tibetan Seamstress" film and some pictures of him on the set of the new film he's written. He's writing another film for Warner Brothers. I miss making movies.

My mom writes about the record-breaking heat in Indiana, how the new shopping center is taking away business from the family's downtown store, and how hard my brother is working. (Subtext: come home.)

Sonny writes at last. Enclosed is a photo of an old woman that she shot in Alabama, where she's been photographing the children of former slaves. We're very similar. She's searching for the essence of things, as I'm trying to do here. Her work is very gutsy and strong. I could ask her to come to Bali, but I know that wouldn't work long term. I have to do this thing in Bali alone, however hard it is.)

So many letters. Hardly anyone even mentions Bali.

Here I am out in the jungle and rice fields of this foreign land. Letters drop in as if from outer space. I recall the faces of friends. I remember my lovers—their scent and the feel of their skin. I am surprised how wistful I am.

"I can feel them, even from here."

"Hey, man, it's okay." Eddie puts his arm around my shoulders. "We're together and we're having a great time, aren't we?"

"Yeah, Eddie, yeah, we are, thanks." I feel better.

We exchange letters, hungry to read English words. I read a letter from his father, a stern man, very displeased that Eddie hasn't taken his final exams. He writes as if he thinks Eddie is still "on break" and fully expects him to return to missionary work. I don't think Eddie has told him his new plans.

Big Swede emerges from the post office. He nods. I wave him over. He joins us for tea. I ask about his girlfriends.

"Don't need them," he says.

"What do you mean?" I ask.

"Spiritual practice is over. We shared *tantric* energies and now we are balanced. My shakti is so great I need two women. Besides, they had to go back to Jakarta," he says, breaking out in laughter.

Eddie, who has been silent, says, "Used them up and threw them away."

Big Swede smiles; it doesn't faze him.

Eddie stomps off across the street to the playing field. I sit with Big Swede for another twenty minutes or so. He's a cool guy; nothing ruffles him. Turns out he's spent a lot of time in India living like a *sadhu*, begging food and living almost naked. He's memorized the entire *Vedas*, thousands of Hindu religious verses. He's been in Bali for five years. A village *dukun* has 'adopted' him in Iseh in East Bali where he's studying lontars.

I feel a hand on my shoulder. I turn. It's Pierre.

"Mail day for you, too?" he asks.

"Yes," I reply.

"Listen, I heard about your camera being stolen. Too bad. But I've got a Bolex you can borrow. I'd like to see you make your movie," he says generously.

"Thanks, that would be great. Maybe next time I come to Sanur I can get it?"

"Sure, anytime. Sorry, I've got to go. I've got a meeting with the minister of tourism. Ciao."

I say goodbye to Swede and catch up with Eddie who is with Dr. Sudarsana, the museum curator. They're looking at an ancient *Rangda* mask. I hurry us out of there. Last time Eddie messed with Rangda, there's was trouble.

Next we go to a Chinese restaurant and pig out. We are hungry. We eat very little of the village food. And drink very little of the water for fear of getting sick. I've lost a lot of weight and frequently have headaches. Probably heat stroke. There's no padding on my butt and my collarbone sticks out.

Eddie is fearless. He'll eat anything. Once, we were eating something and I made the mistake of asking what it was.

"Eel," grinned one of the painters. Sometimes it's better not to ask.

Another time, a Balinese delicacy was served in honor of our arrival in Sindu. It was pig, hairy skin and all—the bristles still on it. No, I don't think so.

As discreetly as possible, I rewrapped the pig in its palm leaf cover and cupped it in my hand. I headed toward the outhouse and when I was sure no one was looking, I pitched it over the compound wall. A couple of dogs greedily fought over it, causing a loud ruckus. Those dogs followed me for days.

Eddie and I go to the market. Hundreds of vendors sell fruit. We try some *durian*, which has a snakelike skin. The taste is very strange, but I grow to like it.

Eddies searches for religious paraphernalia. Sure enough, around to the back and through a smoky haze of incense, are brightly painted umbrellas, baskets, ritual artifacts, costumes. We pick through everything, trying to find out what it's used for.

I buy a box of batteries for our tape recorders (this is getting expensive), some small books and pencils for sketching, and bags of coffee and sugar for Sadia. We also buy a carton of imported Camels for the painters. (Turns out they hate them...too strong.)

We return by bus and bemo. When we get to Sindu, Sadia already knows we talked to Big Swede and Pierre at the post office, what we ate at the warung and the Chinese restaurant, how much money we cashed at the bank, and what we bought at the market. He thanks us for the coffee and sugar before it's unwrapped! How could he know this? Even on a motorbike, they couldn't have rushed back to the village faster than we did.

What they are really excited about is the paper and colored pencils that I bought. Everyone in the village wants some. We give them to the painters and their kids.

"Draw whatever you like. Write the Indonesian and Balinese words below the picture," we say.

Several hundred pieces of paper and colored pencils quickly disappear.

A few days later, the completed drawings return en masse. Snakes, eels, butterflies, bananas, cooking pots, trees, houses, and musical instruments. The styles are incredibly varied: some refined, some rough, some illustrative, some mystical and religious. On each drawing is the name of the object. A wonderful, illustrated Balinese dictionary.

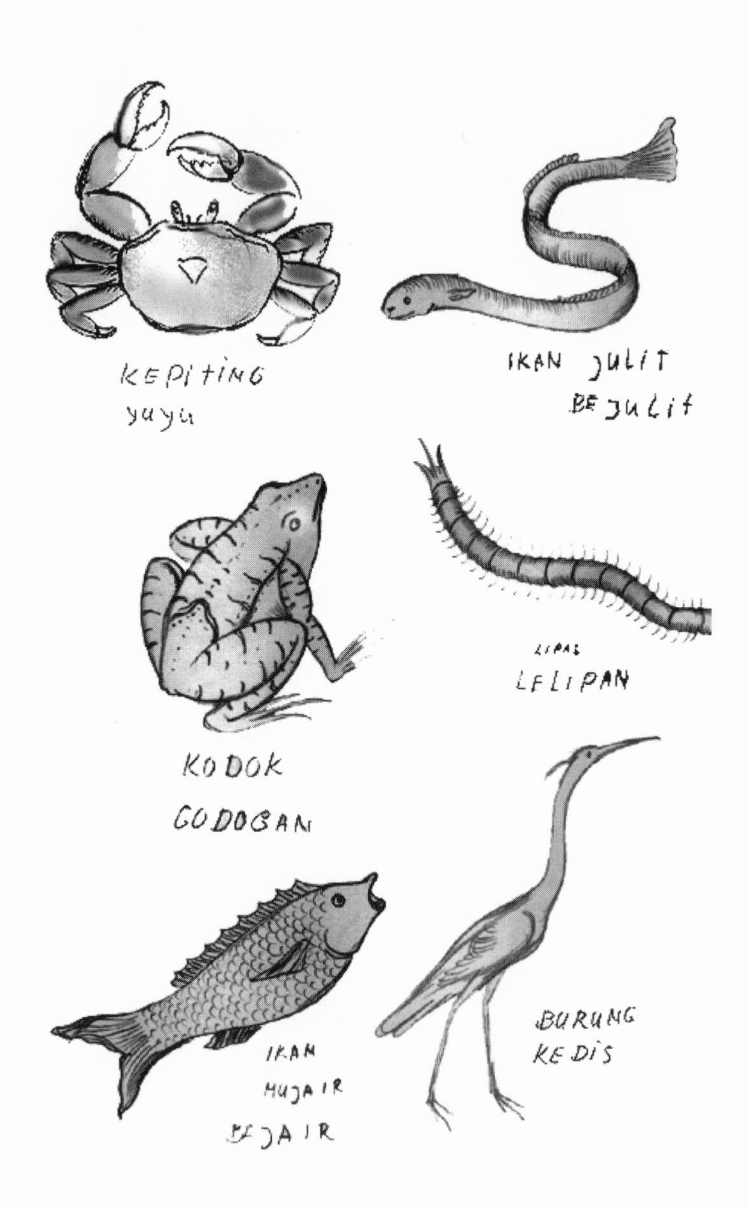
KEPITING
yuyu
IKAN JULIT
BEJULIT
LIPAS
LELIPAN
KODOK
GODOGAN
IKAN
MUJAIR
BEJAIR
BURUNG
KEDIS

Tonight there is a *Topeng* (mask dance theater) in Tobola village nearby. Temple festivals are occasions to dress up. The men wear their best shirts. The women wear new *kabayas* (blouses), their bright orange or black bras showing through the thin, white fabric. It's a great time to take pictures of the women because they are very proud to pose in their new clothes. Eddie and I wear clean shirts and sarongs. Sadia, his wife, and children lead the way. Some painters join us.

It is pitch black. No moon to help us see. Walking down the narrow paths and through the streams is hard enough in the daylight, but at night...one just has to trust. Things slither in the grass under my feet. As I step from the stream, the muddy bank nearly sucks my sandals off. A chorus of frogs begins croaking. Crickets and cicadas deep in the jungle join in. A gamelan of insects.

Lobo takes my hand. He holds on to it. I really don't think about it until he doesn't let go. Here I am, in the middle of a jungle, stars above, wearing a sarong and feeling like this guy's date. But the Balinese men often hold hands with each other, it's no big deal.

Chapter 14

TO MAKE OUR DEMONS FLOW

As we near the temple in the neighboring village, there is the sound of the great gongs. As we get closer, the high-pitched, metallic notes of the gamelan drown out the insect orchestra around us. Gas lanterns create a silhouette effect around the temple. Moths flutter in the air. Bats dive catching insects overhead. We walk through the split doors of the temple. Hundreds of villagers are cheering at two masked clowns dancing in a dusty circle.

A *Topeng* is taking place. This is one of the masked dances that the renowned French actor and playwright Antonin Artaud had seen performed in Paris and had so passionately written about. I read his book, *The Theater & Its Double,* at film school. It was the first time I had even heard of Bali. Not long after Artaud witnessed Balinese theater, he was declared insane and was institutionalized for years.

He wrote that Balinese theater has nothing to do with entertaining people. It is not artificial amusement, or an evening's pastime. Balinese theater goes to the very heart of religious rites. Its goal is to create a spiritual state.

Hardly anyone listened to Artaud because he made the mistake of mocking the surrealists of his day. I feel a kinship with him. I see what he's talking about. Eddie is a big fan of

Artaud's too. He's a voracious reader and is frequently quoting from books he's read.

"Artaud's madness was an asset to his creativity," Eddie says.

Eddie's theory (of Artaud's theory) is that in order to create a transformation of the soul you have to go into the unconscious, getting past your repressions.

"It's not an intellectual thing," he explains. "It's a feeling thing. A ritual. Shared delirium. Dive in head first and bring everyone with you."

There is nervous energy in the air, an expectancy. The crowd stands in a semicircle defining the dusty performance area. Men stand in the back rows; women and children are in the front, closest to the dancers who enter from behind a simple curtain. The gamelan rises and falls with the movements of the dancers, who wear masks ranging from refined to very crude—Balinese archetypes.

Without understanding the dialogue, the play is easy to follow. A prince is traveling through a treacherous landscape to another kingdom in a time of great emergency. His high caste is discernible by his posture, gestures, and refined speech. He commands his buffoon attendants to prepare for battle, then ceremoniously departs behind a curtain. (He changes masks and costume and will reappear as another character later.)

One buffoon is a braggart, loud and fat. The other is tall, skinny, and cautious. When the two cowardly buffoons are left alone in the woods, their real fears come to the surface and their pretenses drop. Are they surrounded by demons and monsters hiding in the shadows? They argue about what to do and end up frightening each other.

Eddie is exuberant. He absolutely loves it.

"Do you see how they've let go? It's not theater as we know it; it's a parallel kind of reality. They enter the world of their ancestors' spirits. It's like going inside a time machine."

When the prince reappears, the buffoons put on courageous airs and respectfully kneel before their master. A mixture of serious drama and burlesque, the topeng has something for everyone.

Eddie continues. "When you are tranced out, you forget yourself, you are enraptured. You are all powerful. Like a god. That's why we are in a temple. Not to appease the gods but to become one. To enter this power."

Ota comes out of the shadows and stands beside Eddie. He is dressed like a priest. His hair and fingernails are long. Eddie gives him a kretek and then lights it for him. He speaks a little English and says something to Eddie, and then points to one of the young girls. Eddie nods his head and laughs.

I leave them and join the villagers at the warung at the back of the temple for tea. Most of the teenagers have congregated here. The girls stick together, moving about in twos and threes, flirting with the boys from the safety of a group. A fascinating ritual, the same all over the world.

Some kids yell, "Darimani, Tuan?"

Proudly, I shout back, "Sindu."

A *wayang kulit* is next. I watch from both sides of the screen as the *dalang* manipulates the puppets and their shadows against the screen while channeling their voices. Occasionally one of the puppets held over the dalang's head smashes against the oil lamp, emitting a shower of sparks and a puff of smoke. This adds danger and magic to the night air.

I look around. This is one of the few times no one pays attention to me. They have entered the shadow world. A young woman looks over, brushes the hair from her face, then smiles. Moments pass, we lock eyes. I hold my breath, hoping to freeze the moment. Then she looks away. Wow.

I am back in my tiny room. It must be 2:00 or 3:00 A.M. "Big Buzz" made his midnight flight hours ago. Through the wall I hear Ota give Eddie a mask. I lay back into the bed and listen to Eddie as he dances around the porch, trying to find a voice to fit the mask.

Later, the room is quiet except for the crickets, frogs, lizards, and beasts of the jungle. I hold the look of the young woman in my mind, as I fall into sleep.

The land has been cleared for our house. As I survey the site, Sadia arrives. He's got his sad smile on.

"Australian bad man," he mumbles. "Not get money."

Sadia learned of a Sindu Painting Exhibition in Sydney, but never heard from the Australian nor received any money. Sadia had given him many fine paintings, and he is once again worried how he will get money to buy paints and canvas for the painting commune.

"Selling paintings to tourists is ultimately destructive," says Eddie. "Eventually, they'll just want the birds and the more decorative stuff. And that's what everyone will paint. The cultural power of the paintings will be lost."

"Eddie! Not now," I say.

I feel guilty that the painters were ripped off by a white man. Sadia is so trusting, so open, so easy to exploit. I should have seen it coming. This is my chance to do something.

"Don't worry, I think I can help you," I say.

"Bagus!" he says loosening up. "Always like this in Bali. Good come from bad."

"Also bad things come from good," I add.

"Yaaa, but if bad, it's okay. God gives us bad thing so that we can learn be better person."

Whatever the situation, Sadia's philosophy seems to always bring him into a better frame of mind.

The curator at the San Francisco Art Center will flip out over the Balinese paintings and probably want to do a show.

"If they know what they are looking at, it will have more meaning."

I write descriptions and stories for each painting. I've already compiled a mailing list of wealthy patrons who attended our movie premiere. Adrian can send it to the Art Center. Within three weeks, everything was in motion, and about 100 paintings were being air expressed "collect" to the Art Center.

Dawn.

"Nipas, Nipas!" the painters shout out, laughing.

Very funny. Jeez, Louise, don't they know I just got to bed? I stayed up all night, mulling over an idea. I can't wait to tell Sadia.

It's barely light. How can they see to paint?

Sadia hands me a cup of coffee. I blurt out my idea.

"Let's organize a Balinese theater troupe and tour the world! Like they did in the 30s'."

I'm two minutes into the conversation when Eddie challenges me.

"You'd take them out of the village, break up families? Expose them to disease?"

"I've thought of that, Eddie. We'll take the whole village intact, men, women, and children. They'll cook their own food and we'll bring a healer too," I counter.

"And a very large painting exhibition can go too," says Sadia.

"Of course. We'll put together a multitalented ensemble. Each person alternates between *gamelan, topeng,* or *wayang.* We'll do more with less."

"It's a tourist performance," says Eddie.

"No, it will be classical Balinese dance and music. The older traditional stuff that's fading out. It will renew interest here. It's brilliant."

Eddie shakes his head, but I'm on a roll.

"Not only that, but musicians and dancers in other countries can play with the gamelan in special workshops. It will be a multi cultural musical celebration!"

"Aren't you forgetting something?"

"What?"

"The draft?"

"When it goes to America, I'll skip ahead to set up the next country."

"Tourism is the very thing that is destroying Bali. You know that, don't you?" he says sourly.

"Eddie this isn't tourism..."

"Yes! Yes, it is. It will speed up interest in Bali and bring more tourists. You want to be responsible for that?"

"Eddie, look, it's a cultural exchange, it's..."

"I'm really disappointed in you. Of all people, I thought you understood." Eddie storms off.

Sadia has never seen us argue before.

I go into my room and start writing. I can hear Eddie grumbling on and on.

I write to a long-time musician friend and his wife.

Dear Deke and Margo,

... Did you get the tape I sent? It may need equalizing because it's hard to hear the incredible range of the orchestra—the piercing highs and thundering lows. Please play it for everyone. Turn them on. See if you can get a record deal.

This is top secret. I want to bring a fifty-piece Balinese orchestra and theater group on a world tour. I'll premiere the film we're making at the same time to boost publicity.

When it's in the States, I want you to bring the gamelan into a studio and produce an album with Western electric and acoustic instruments, Latin American, and primitive instruments. The important thing is to get musicians from all over the world to play with each other and learn.

I really need your help. I thought Eddie would help me with this but I don't think it will work out. He thinks it will harm Bali. Too much sun! Please write today.

Love, Nick

PS. Please destroy this letter when you've read it.

I'm still shook up from my argument with Eddie. I get up and go to shave. I talk to myself in the mirror. And there she is again.

She is lovely, with long, black silky, hair. Maybe eighteen. I speak to her in the mirror. "Salamat pagi." She nods. She looks upset too.

"I'm all upset. Eddie hates the world tour idea. Am I doing the right thing? I think it would help Bali. What I'm suppose to do here?"

Surprisingly, she responds by shaking her head solemnly from side to side. She seems very unhappy. This is too weird. How can...? I turn and look behind me and she's not there. Of course. I look back in the mirror and see her walk away. I look behind me again. No one.

My heart is pounding like crazy. Does she knows what's going on? No. My mind is playing tricks on me because I am so worked up.

I go into Eddie's room and tell him what happenned.

"Messages, messages? What do you think it means?" he says sullenly.

I go back to my room and reread the letter on the bed. It frightens me. This is exactly what I do <u>not</u> want to do. I want to live here. That's all. I don't have to <u>do</u> anything.

I don't have to try to package my Balinese experience for export. I hate myself for the inability to just "be."

But I can't help myself. I love this place so much I want to share it. Who do I know besides Eddie who really gets it?

No one. A touring performance would be exciting—a flash, a spectacle.

Would it really speed up the demise of what I cherish? I don't think so. But why am I so compelled to always have to make something?

Confused, I lay down and listen to the painters and dream.

The sound of the painters laughing creates ripples on the surface of a still ocean which become millions of tiny, pulsating bubbles. Waves wash them onto the beach and then recede. On the sand is my mirror. The girl is no longer in it. She is dancing for me in the surf with complete abandon. She smiles and tosses her head.

On the beach are dozens of children, more and more appear, and begin to wade into the surf to join her. The children disappear as they enter the water, and only the girl and I remain.

A cloud passes and the sun streaks down. I walk toward the girl. She reaches for me. I am excited and afraid. She is almost transparent. She is covered with fish scales, not quite human. She touches me and my whole body shivers, pulsates, and explodes into pure energy. My consciousness moves through the energy fields until the sounds bring reality back.

Sadia is talking to me. He says something about the house. I think he's apologizing. Different craftsmen will come soon, but right now they are busy elsewhere.

He smiles. "Don't worry. New house is coming."

Eddie says Ota is coming over. He's made a magic amulet that will help Eddie get a girl.

"Now you're into magic amulets?" I snap.

"Guaranteed to work like a charm! Maybe you ought to get one so you can catch the girl in the mirror," he says covertly.

Just then Ota arrives. He walks with a gnarled cane. A Balinese calendar is rolled under his arm.

Ota sits down with us. He explains the various symbols on the calendar. There's a coconut tree, an upside-down demon, a broken hoe, an elephant-fish, a cremation tower, a broken boat, a decapitated head, a dragon, and many other strange images. Ota points to the decapitated head which is being held at bay in a treetop by two men with spears. One is trying to kill it.

Ota says, "Begoong is not bad spirit. Somebody think bad. But not bad. Begoong is destroyer, go away old sick things, then come new. Begoong spirit come when burn rice field. Make way for new. You understand?"

Ota wipes his wispy beard with the corner of his white sarong. Eddie is taking notes. He loves this stuff. Ota mutters something in Balinese. Eddie tells me that I have to leave now. Ota is about to give him the charm and say a mantra, and this must be done in private.

Chapter 15

Menari Demam
DANCE FEVER

Days later. I am too sick to paint. Ota sits in the pavilion polishing a mask. Eddie is fascinated.

"If you make a good house, someone will want to inhabit it," cackles Ota.

He hands the mask to Eddie who puts it on, then stomps up the dust, twirling around, dramatically shifting his weight, in front of the hut. Ota is pleased.

"Pandai! Pandai!

Eddie is getting really good. Ota stands behind him and moves his arms so that he can feel the right position. Feel the right position. I like that.

Lobo clangs on the *gangsa,* pulverizing my feverish head. Must we? Eddie shows off his new moves. A small crowd has gathered. Eddie loves a crowd. A determined look on his face, he rolls his eyes backward—trancelike.

My weakness and on-again-off-again illness is pulling me down. Sadia sends me to Wayan Linah, the local *dukun* (medicine man) whom we see from time to time. He lives a few kilometers away in Iseh. Turns out he is the one who 'adopted' Big Swede and gave him the name "Ida Bagus."

When I approach the mud walls of his compound, three vicious dogs hold me at bay. A small round woman with bright shiny eyes (his wife?) chases the dogs away. She leads me to a thatched roof pavilion at the center of the compound. Big Swede is sitting in the lotus position in another pavilion, meditating.

Wayan Linah sits on a mattress surrounded by lontars, offerings, and clothing. It looks like an outdoor bedroom. The air is heavy with burning incense. Smiling, his arms outstretched, he's glad to see me.

"Nipas, Nipas," he says. "Are you *sakit* (sick)?"

He knows why I am here. He looks in my eyes, rubs his fingers across my skin, and smells me. He holds onto my arm. His wife prepares *obat* (a sticky paste), which he paints on my forehead.

"You have monkey mind," he tells me. "You know monkey? Always worry. You must be happy. We can meditate together."

I like this guy. No wonder Swede stays here. There's a lot to learn from such a willing teacher. We have an immediate rapport. He's bright, and between English and Indonesian, we do fine. He asks me if I'll photograph his wife. The tiny woman sits absolutely still and expressionless until after the shutter snaps, then she bursts into a huge smile.

A line of sick Balinese people are patiently waiting to be healed. He says there is an unusual wave of headaches in the village.

"Many people *sakit kepala,* you understand?"

Wayan is in no hurry to end our conversation, but I'm embarrassed to take so much of his time when others are waiting. I excuse myself. Big Swede finishes his meditation with a laugh. He accompanies me to the compound door.

"You don't look so good, I'll walk you back."

When we arrive, I invite Swede in for some coffee and food. Eddie meets us at the gate.

"Linah's a balian *weseda*?", Eddie asks Swede.

"Yeah."

"He gets his knowledge from books, from the lontars. You can't get real power from reading! A balian *taksu* goes into trance," boasts Eddie.

"Both have different duties," explains Swede.

"But a balian *taksu* has much more power," argues Eddie. "They know magic!"

"If you're talking about Ota, you're mistaken. He's a mask carver, not a dukun."

"You don't know that."

"I know he dresses like a dukun and fools around with black magic," he says twisting a finger on his forehead. "Be careful, he doesn't put a spell on you Eddie," Swede laughs.

"Maybe you're the one who should be careful," replies Eddie. "Why don't you go back to Iseh? You don't know shit about this village. This is my village." Eddie turns on his heels and goes in the compound.

"I'll skip the coffee. Another time," says Swede.

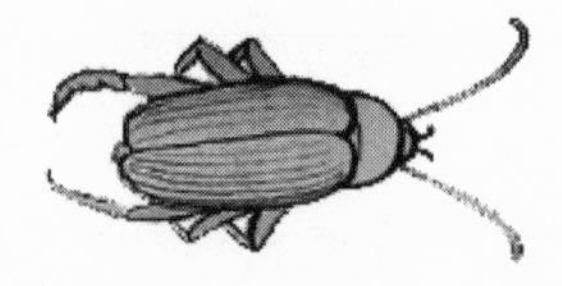

Night. Back at the hut. Eddie starts talking again about finding a Balinese wife, as he rubs a small, white-cloth pouch that hangs from a string necklace around his neck. It's about the size of a small box of matches. Kawi letters are written on the bag.

"From Ota. It's a love charm. Inside are fish eyes, perfumes, oils, and herbs." Then he quickly wraps it back up.

"Full moon night is the best time to use this charm. You can be my best man." He laughs and returns to his room. Bali brings out a whole side of Eddie I've never seen before.

I lie on my bed and recall how rich the day has been. When we first entered the village, dozens of unknown faces surrounded us. Now we are learning names and making many friends.

I play the tapes I've recorded of the shadow play. The magical shadows revisit my mind as I listen to the trancelike singing of the dalang. I recall my enchantment, the tales of hideous monsters, brave and ethical princes, beautiful princesses, long journeys into magical kingdoms, gods, clowns, and great battles. I've only been here a few months and already I am worlds away. The penetration into this magical land has begun. I feel it's time to begin our film.

Through the wall I say, "Let's start our film. Our senses are wide open and everything is still new."

"We have film, but no camera. Remember?" asks Eddie.

"We'll borrow Devaux's."

"Not me," refuses Eddie.

"I don't know any other camera in Bali that works. Do you?"

No answer.

Chapter 16

PAINTING MYSELF INTO A CORNER

"Nipas, Nipas," clamor my human alarm clocks. Malaria? The dizziness and weakness return. I have trouble waking up. I have trouble sleeping. I'm exhausted from the intensity. It's very tiring to live in another language.

Weakly, I sit with the painters and work. My head. *Ke-thump, ke-thump thump, ke-thump.* It feels like bolts of lightning striking my head every few seconds.

Lobo brings me some bananas and tea. I am sick of being sick. Village life requires a strong constitution, something I admittedly don't have. The food, the organisms in the water and air, the sleep cycle, the heat during the day, all take their toll. We drink no water, only tea, which has been boiled. Dysentery is a fact of life. Still, I'd rather be sick here than well anywhere else.

The painters want me to paint. Why not? I had a few painting classes at the Art Center. With difficulty, I sit on the bamboo mats with my small empty canvas in my lap. My butt is now just bones. I've lost another five pounds.

Rani is one of the more accomplished painters. He paints a large canvas filled with frogs which look like him. Lobo paints butterflies and birds.

Others paint jungle landscapes: a Ramayana battle; Hanuman, the monkey king, fighting demons. Sadia paints a meditating Buddha mandala. His technique is primitive and powerful.

I paint a Buddha too. Well, not a Buddha really — it's more like a *Schmoo*, only Oriental, sitting in meditation, with many arms held up by four tamed beasts. I put magical artifacts in the mystical Schmoo's hands. I proudly show off my work. They look at me askance.

Rani ask, "*Apa itu*?" (What is that?) and points at the Schmoo.

I answer, "*Tidak tau.*" (I don't know.)

Not a good answer. Sadia explains that paintings evoke a spirit. You should know what you're painting. It's either Rama, or Sita, or Hanuman, or the Buddha, or animals.

"It's dangerous not to know," Sadia warns.

"Maybe a leyak will enter your mind. You must concentrate on something."

Sadia says that from now on I must know what I paint.

Damn it, I've got critters. Lice or crabs have taken up residence in the hair on my arms and legs. They itch terribly. They are too small to pick off and have burrowed under my skin. The painters think this is one of the funniest things they've ever seen. Even Sadia chuckles. Give me a break. No one offers a remedy; no, that would spoil their fun. What do the Balinese do?

I practice gamelan for a while until the batteries in the tape recorder wear out. I collect all the batteries and put them in the sun, hoping to recharge them. It only gives enough juice for another minute. Between the scratching and the bad batteries, this has been a tough day.

Eddie and I go to the Denpasar market and stock up on tubes of paint, kretek cigarettes and, as always, batteries.

Eddie says, "You're spending a fortune on batteries for the tape recorder. Electricity should be as free as the sun. What if we could generate it ourselves? Wouldn't that be great?"

Then we go to the museum and return a book I'd borrowed from Dr. Surdasana, the museum curator. He tells me to put coconut oil on my critters. In a few hours, the itching subsides.

We stop at the post office.

Dear Nick,

... You sound worn out. Take a rest from village life. Go to the beach. Get laid.

I'm afraid I can't come to Bali. We are busy editing my new film. The draft board is still looking for you. I told them you were in Germany. Ha! Can't you sneak back into the country somehow? I've got lots of new investors. And money! We can do our film at last!

Adrian

Next stop. Sanur. We go to the Bali Hai Hotel for lunch. Afterwards, I'll go to see Pierre Devaux at The World Bank office upstairs.

A row of Balinese woman greet us with flowers as we enter. Eddie slinks through the lobby like a wet dog coiled in gloom. He plays word games loud enough for tourists to hear.

"Confusion, delusion, abusing," catching a rich woman's eye, "What?" You don't like those words? They're English words. How 'bout decay, moray, what'cha say?"

The tourists turns away quickly. Eddie stays on her.

"Can't keep from dying. Can't keep from trying. Can't keep from sighing."

I am about to scold him, but Eddie gives me a look and says, "Can you see me? Can you save me? Beautiful sir?"

The hotel gives me the creeps.

"Hey, let's get a hamburger," I suggest, trying to lighten his mood and recall earlier times.

Our dirty feet and wrinkled faded sarongs turn a few heads as we enter the coffee shop. We have that white man's graveyard look. Hamburgers are very expensive—about $2.50 in U.S. dollars. That's enough money for a week of meals in the village. What are we doing here? We are betraying the village, spending money like this. And we are renegging our promise to ourselves to live like the Balinese. We leave without paying the bill.

We go through the beachside entrance of the hotel and stop by the pool. Eddie pushes a finger down his throat until it touches the back and he gags. The hamburger pieces come up and spill out into the pool. Eddie grins. I do the same. Sweet revenge.

Eddie won't 'grovel' to Pierre. Fine. But someone has to see him if we are to borrow his camera.

His third-story office is filled with maps, charts, and studies. While I wait for Pierre, I pick up a blue folder which is titled, *Executive Summary: Tourism Development in Bali, 1970-1980.* I skim through the document. It is an extensive plan that shows how Bali could accommodate and service 500,000 tourists a year. It's detailed down to how many new jobs there will have to be, what they are, how the electricity and water will be provided, and includes investment returns which are staggering.

I look out the window and peer into a family compound from above. A woman sweeps the ground and then places an offering. I shudder at how much the island will change.

There are already 10,000 tourists a year and that's 9,998 too many for me. I find myself ignoring Westerners on the street. I don't want to share Bali with those who are here to lie on the beach, get drunk, and go home. There is little respect for what this island is really all about. It's a cheap vacation.

I hear Pierre coming from the other room. I express my concern for Balinese values.

"Won't they simply be overrun like Hawaii?"

Pierre shrugs it off. "If you really want to help your village friends," he says bluntly, "you'll teach them English so they can work in the hotels."

I remind him about his offer to loan us the camera. He apologizes that the camera isn't really his but belongs to the World Bank.

"I can't just loan it to you, but perhaps I could 'rent' it," he suggests.

"We don't have much money left."

"Hmm, what about allowing us to make copies of any footage you shoot?"

"What do you want it for?" I ask.

He says he'll probably never really want any footage but that the agreement will protect him from his superiors, and I'll get a camera I can use. His secretary types up a little agreement. I feel a little sick when I sign it.

By the time Eddie returns from his walk, it's already too late to get a bemo back. Pierre drives us back to Sideman, a village within easy walking distance from Sindu. Eddie is pleased we have a movie camera again. I don't tell him about the agreement.

On the way, the jeep waits for a parade of ducks to cross the road. On both sides are high, mud walls with houses hidden behind them. Only a few feet away there is a large crack where many bricks have fallen, which allows me to see in. On the other side of the wall are three generations of Balinese women. They don't see me. The grandmother's comb pulls smoothly through the raven-black hair of her daughter, whose child sleeps in her mother's long arms.

Bare-breasted and beautiful. Dark-bronze skin, wrapped in batik sarongs. The low sun throws a trio of halos in the rising dust behind them. These Balinese women—perfect! Quiet, gentle, touching. I nudge Eddie, who looks in. The younger woman hums a soft lullaby.

"Messages, messages," we both say at the same time.

The vision evokes the possibilities for our film: The Women of Bali.

The next day Eddie supervises the painters as they prepare a large gray canvas for the backdrop. Sadia arranges for women from the village to be our subjects. We will re-create the vision we saw together and combine it with dance.

One by one—girls, adolescents, women, and elders sit before the camera. Eddie directs; I operate the camera. Sadia's oldest son holds a white canvas near the faces to reflect light. Eddie tries to direct a mood on the face of each between innocence and wisdom, like those we saw on the faces of Ardja dancers. Most are very nervous and freeze before the camera. After about a dozen attempts with different women, we stop. This isn't working.

There is a murmur from among the crowd of people who watch behind us. Wayan Linah, the *dukun* from Iseh, enters. Politely, he pulls me aside. He knows we are having trouble.

"Nipas, maybe they are afraid for their souls," he suggests, smiling.

We hadn't thought of this.

"What should we do?" I ask.

"Did you bless your *bioskop*?" the medicine man asks. "I can with my holy water." Great idea.

In front of everyone, he sprinkles holy water on the camera. He whispers a throaty mantra and pastes flower petals on the camera and tripod, then one on our foreheads between our eyebrows for "the ability to see God." Immediately, the tension leaves the situation.

The first girl sits down in front of the camera. Eddie slowly moves like an Ardja dancer and calls forth the desired emotion. He says, "Ardja face," and points to his expression. Almost immediately, she mirrors the desired interpretation and I'm able to film it. This quickly becomes a game, and every girl and woman tries to top the last one. Eddie gets more and more into directing through his own dance. He has found the emotional chord and rides it out, evoking, awakening, and drawing it out from his subjects. Everyone is having fun, and we are banking great stuff. Innocence transforming to sensuality, changing to higher wisdom, and back to child-like grace. Truly amazing.

We are so pleased with the performances that we hug each other. Everyone cheers.

The next day Sadia takes a collection of paintings to Jakarta. It's his first plane ride and the first time in his life that he's been away from Bali. We share a bemo with him and get off in Denpasar. He goes on to the airport. I hope he'll be all right.

We take our exposed black-and-white film to Cheng for processing. When we get there, we pass a governmental dignitary and his entourage. They stare at us strangely. Inside, Cheng has just finished their formal portait. There is an elegant velvet chair, some palms, a carpet, and a cloud backdrop. Very formal. Eddie loves it.

"Shoot one of me, Cheng!", says Eddie, sitting in the chair in a Sergei Eisenstein pose.

Cheng loads in a sheet of film and looks through the large view camera.

"It's a five-second exposure, so please keep still."

But Eddie doesn't. Keeping his head still, he slowly moves his arms. Cheng is about to take out the film.

"No, wait, shoot another on the same film."

"A double exposure?" asks Cheng.

"Yes, yes, it will be great," exclaims Eddie.

We hang out and drink tea while Cheng develops and prints the photo. We talk to him through his darkroom door. He comes out and presents Eddie with the photo of two Eddies, one angelic and still, the other, a blurred and distorted face pulling away from the body.

"Who's this?" I point to the grimacing face.

"My evil twin!" laughs Eddie.

Eddie goes off to the market to buy God knows what. He's doing wacky and wackier things when we come to town. I wait for him in the Chinese restaurant when I run into Pierre. He asks how the filming went. Excitedly, I tell him all about the women we filmed and how great I think the footage is.

"It really captures the innocence and playfulness of these people."

I tell him that I am going to send it to the States for processing. He says he can send it by diplomatic pouch to Australia and get it processed much faster. He'll even pay for it. I take the two rolls from my shoulder bag and give them to him.

Just then, Eddie walks in. "What the hell are you doing?!!"

I explain that Pierre is going to develop the film for us in Australia.

"And then?" challenges Eddie.

"And then he's going to make a copy and return the original."

"You've what?" shouts Eddie.

"It's our agreement."

"What agreement?" Eddie blasts a look at me.

"In exchange for renting the camera," says Devaux. Eddie goes into an absolute fit.

"Whose side are you on? You are going to give this guy our footage? Behind my back?!"

He storms out of the restaurant. I chase after him and grab his arm.

"Eddie, calm down, it's only a copy. I had to. You refused to come. I <u>had</u> to make that deal. How else was I going to get us a camera? It's still our footage." He pulls away, huffs off down the main drag, and gets lost in the crowd.

Night. Eddie is still pissed. I should have told him. I walk around the Denpasar night market. It's loud. It stinks. It's dusty.

I stay at the Adi Yasa losmen. It is loud. It stinks. It's dusty.

How is it I find myself here when I have a village to live in? But then to actually sit on a toilet! Ahh!!! No pigs sniffing around. No roosters.

I write letters to Adrian and my folks. I'm gaining insights into myself but quickly losing touch with the outside world.

The stuffy night air is like a heavy wool blanket. I sleep without a sarong. There are no windows to open and no breeze. I read Sonny's letter before falling asleep.

> Dear Nicholas,
>
> ... Jung says, "synchronistic events almost invariably accompany crucial phases of individuation." If your days are filled with magical connections, then congratulations! Stay awake, pay attention....
>
> Love, Sonny

Chapter 17

ASHES, ASHES, WE ALL FALL DOWN

Late morning. On the way back to the village, I see Ota and Eddie sitting at a warung off the main road. Eddie shows Ota the double-exposure photograph. Both are drinking arak and laughing. Their backs are to me. They don't see me approach.

"This is strong power," Ota says, holding the photo and pointing to the double image with his long fingernail.

"Good, huh?" says Eddie.

"Must get more power. I show you how to make the mind strong, so spirit can leave the body.

"Yeah. You want to help Bali because your spirit is Balinese. You are ancestor come back in Western body." Just then, Ota glances my way and stops talking.

"Pagi," I nod.

"Pagi," says Ota.

I don't like what I hear.

Eddie hands me a recent edition of *Time* magazine that he got in Denpasar.

"Thought you'd want to see this," he says soberly.

The first thing I read is:

> "Students who bomb and burn are criminals. Police and National Guardsmen who needlessly shoot or assault students are criminals. All who applaud these criminal acts share in their evil. We must declare a national cease-fire...."

Eddie looks over at me.

"No, the next page."

I turn the page.

> "The island republic of Singapore recently proclaimed itself "a bastion of resistance to the social pollution of hippies." Last week, after Singapore police arrested three long-haired youths from neighboring Malaysia, the young men were held in jail for seventeen hours until they consented to being given short haircuts...."

"No, no. One more," he says.

Then I see it. Janis Joplin and Jimi Hendrix are dead — both from overdoses! Shit! Janis use to come to our studio between sets at the Matrix. I met Jimi at Monterey Pop. Offstage they were both insecure and a bit lost, but it didn't matter, onstage they pushed past it. They were brave. They were passion embodied.

Eddie says, "They went for it."

"Yeah. They did."

The three of us get up and sadly walk into the village.

The slow, deep-toned thumps from the *kulkul* in the banyan tree signal a cremation. Synchronicity again.

The village has waited six years for the right day and to have enough money to cremate their dead. In the graveyard we watch as as twenty bodies are dug up and the bones washed.

A cremation will insure that the souls of their relatives join with God. It's a celebratory day and the final responsibility for their loved ones who have passed over. For me, it's a sad day.

We change into our fine sarongs and saputs and go to the cemetary of the dead. The families have all gathered together in an area of raised platforms. Many families we know have dead that they will release today.

I think of Janis and Jimi.

"End of an era, death of a dream," murmurs Eddie.

"No, Janis and Jimi may be dead, but the dream is alive here, and it's our job to bring it back home somehow."

The families clean the bones, arrange offerings, then wrap it all in grass mats. These mats are loaded into large papier-mâché tiger, fish, and bull effigies which are then carried by dozens of frenzied men and boys who shout, spin, turn, and twist, while running and carrying the animals to the cremation towers. I almost get run over by the crazed procession.

"We must confuse the spirit so it will not be able to find its way back to the village to haunt us," Sadia says.

The women carry more offerings and pass them to priestss, who arrange them on the cremation towers. Then fire is set to fifteen towers, and the village gathers around to watch. Dark-black smoke rises from charring animals. The stench of death is appalling. I have to cover my mouth to keep from getting sick.

Chapter 18

THE CHILDREN'S CLUB

Morning light. Smell of paint, as I move colors around my canvas and watch how they blend. Afternoon light. The weight of the heat pushes my face into the bamboo mats, as I drift among the legs and arms of the painters. Do we dream the same dreams as we nap? As it cools, crisp, sharp notes enter my mind from the gamelan, as Lobo adds pattern after pattern, until my head can hold no more, it's into deep swirling waters which chill and awaken me. Now I'm ready for the eyes and ears and layers of laughter coming, going, echoing. I'm guided down blackened village paths. We enter an ancient temple. Pattern saronged figures, offerings held high, incense, fire, chanting elders, and shouting masks. Days and days, moments of heat and chill, of light and dark, blur and swirl together. Timeless worlds and sensations.

Today is the day we start building our house! We carry twenty-foot bamboo poles from Sideman, a neighboring village. Heavy suckers. It's not easy to walk with them on my shoulders. No problem for the Balinese. And no problem for Eddie. Where does he get his strength?

We stack them on the plot where the house is to be built. The once-overgrown land has already been cleared. Every plant has been gently pulled up. Nothing is wasted. Each has its own use. I shoot lots of film to show the interconnectedness of the Balinese with nature.

We help carry dense, black stones for the foundation from the ruined temple (where we bathed). It's a long way. I can only carry the small ones. Eddie carries large ones and laughs and jokes with the others on the way. I heave and gasp.

Having temple stones for the foundation of the house makes me feel good. Sadia's wife and the priest carefully erect an altar in a corner of the site and thank the gods for the life of the bamboo, the stones, and the plants. Offerings will also be made in Sadia's family temple during the construction of the house. You can't be too careful. When in doubt, make an offering.

After dinner when the air has cooled, Sadia leads me through the dark along the main path. He says he has a surprise. I feel the hot bark of an unseen Bali dog as it snaps at my heels. Someone throws a stone. A yelp, and the animal runs off.

A hand slips into mine. I can't see whose it is or where we are going, but it is reassuring. We arrive at the main temple.

Gamelan practice! Thirty or so instruments are arranged around a one-walled open pavilion. There are many genders like the one in my hut—but of various sizes. Each has an octave or so of bronze keys. Many of the painters hammer away at the keys as if there were no tomorrow.

Several large gongs are struck infrequently, every sixty-four beats. Two drums, male and female, signal tempo changes.

Two flutes play interlocking melodies. The flutists use circular breathing to keep the air going through the flutes without interruption; the music never pauses for a breath.

Four seated men play a *reyong,* a long instrument of twelve, overturned bronze bowls—large ones on the left, and small ones on the right. Eight arms—resembling a human octopus—strike the bowl tops quickly, producing a hearty, rippling sound.

Dozens of boys stand or sit along the temple wall and listen. (The village has three gamelan clubs—children's, young men's, and old men's.) This is the young men's group. I call them "the rockers."

Moths fly around suspended oil lamps. *Tjetjaks,* huge lizards with suction-cupped toes, stick to the walls and ceiling of the pavilion. Every so often a tjetjak's tongue will snatch an insect from the air. A quick chomp, and the bug is history. The music is a perfect accompaniment for the moth-hunting lizards.

Sadia's surprise is that I can join the group. Wow!

A boy leaves his instrument. Lobo smiles, a kretek dangling from his lips. He motions to me to sit down. Thirty pairs of eyes watch me. The tempo is very fast, too fast. I can't find a place to jump in. The drummer slaps the drum and the group slows down. I begin to play—not too fast, not too loud. As I go over the pattern a few times, my confidence builds. I take my eyes away from my hands and look up. Lobo approves. The drums pick up the pace and we are cookin', carried in a current of pure sensation. We are many; we are one. Damn, this is great!

I close my eyes and see cells dividing, ferns unfolding, clouds forming, ripples rising on a pond, vibrations, harmony, the source of creation, energy before matter.

Suddenly, a pause in the pattern. I slip up, but quickly recover. I'm back. We slow down; we speed up. Then, an abrupt stop—chang! chang! pock! and the final strike on the lowest gong which rings out in the night until only the insects are heard. Tremendous.

My friends laugh. Some change instruments. Others take a break and light up kreteks. A large tjetjak greedily chomps another moth.

How did I get here? This place is so far from my childhood in Indiana. I never had a desire to travel until the draft. Then suddenly, I had to leave. It could have been Canada, or anywhere but it was Asia that drew me; first by her music. Now I've come to know the extraordinary people who play it. I feel that I belong here. I'm ready to remake myself. We are slowly losing or leaving our possessions and getting by with very little. Sinking in, surrendering.

A boy takes over my instrument. It's his turn. I listen for an hour as the gamelan rehearses new pieces. The oil lamp throws shadows on the wall. The choppy pounding of mallets makes the musicians look like Santa's helpers frenetically finishing gifts the night before Christmas.

Night-blooming flowers fill the air with an intoxicating scent. A chorus of insects and barking dogs fills the quiet between compositions. When "the rockers" finish, the kids who have been hanging around the edges of the pavilion grab up the still-warm mallets and claim their instruments. It's time for the next generation of players to practice.

Lobo walks me back along the path to Sadia's compound and my room. I am glad it is dark when my eyes fill up. I don't want him to see how moved I am.

The next day passes quickly. I sleep through most of it. Tonight the gamelan will practice again. I am too dizzy to sit up. This sickness comes and goes when I least expect it. It's a drag. Ota comes to the compound to get Eddie. They go off somewhere together. I can hear the music coming from the temple. I wish I were there.

The crickets, frogs, and other creatures make sounds of their own, first from one side of the village and then the other. The insect sounds wash through me like massive electronic waves. Insect communication? Maybe gamelan comes from these natural sounds and rhythms. Everything vibrates. I've just been too busy to notice. The music is everywhere. As I fall asleep, "Big Buzz" flies through my consciousness.

The sound of Big Buzz creates a wave of flickering light that passes through golden trees. I am standing in a forest. The girl in the mirror appears. Behind her is Gunung Agung. She puts her hands together, falls to the ground in prayer, and disappears into the earth. I put my hands on the warm ground where she knelt.

I awaken from the dream and realize I am back in the room. I close my eyes in hopes of seeing her again.

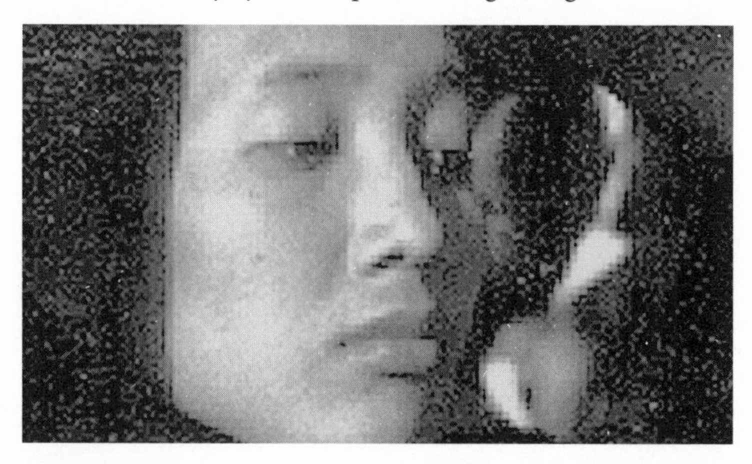

"Look, look, look!" shouts Eddie, as he leaps in the air.

"There's another one!" A huge red-and-black dragonfly swoops down and then careens back into the air above.

"Wow! Did you see that one?" screams Eddie. Eddie and I love dragonflies. One of the kids puts sticky glue on the end of a long pole, hoists it in the air, catches the dragonfly, and pops it in his bag. Later we eat them. Crunchy. They are more fun to watch than eat.

It's bath time. The painters join us for a dip in "Tom Sawyer's swimmin' hole." The women's bathing spot is crowded as well. Everyone is getting ready for tonight's big temple ceremony. It is an *odalan* (birthday) for a temple in Sidakaria village.

At the temple, there is an *Ardja* dance, a comedic opera.

Very pretty dancers wear towering flower headpieces and sing high-pitched, nasal melodies. Their hands coil in and out of mudra positions, as they scold or chastise each other. Their eyes dart from side to side, balancing between innocence and worldliness, between girlhood and womanhood. It's too dark for pictures unless I use the flash. I shoot one shot, and the flash is so disruptive I vow never to use it again.

On the sidelines, three young Ardja dancers from our village critique the dancers' makeup and movements, alternately praising or envying every move with their glances. In the shadows against the temple walls, teenage boys observe the girls.

Last night's Ardja gamelan has caused a stir among Sindu's gamelan club. An argument ensues. Many think Sidakaria's gamelan sounds better.

Lobo is fascinated by my tape recorder and wants to borrow it. He loves the *bagus* little machine that captures the gamelan. I show him how to use it.

In the morning, Lobo returns the tape recorder with the tape still inside. Eddie and I listen to it. What we reconstruct from the recorded tape is a real hoot. Lobo sneaks out to a neighboring village and surreptitiously records their gamelan rehearsal to capture the tuning and compositions.

Apparently he forgot to turn the tape recorder off, because we hear him return home. The first thing he does is sing a lullaby to his baby boy. He, like every Balinese man or woman, loves his children dearly.

That afternoon, many of the men in the gamelan come by and ask to listen to the tape. There is much discussion. The gist of it is that Sindu's instruments are in desperate need of tuning. Sadia asks me for 10,000 rupiah (a few dollars) to get the gamelan tuned. I am glad to be able to help.

It's a very big deal when, a few days later, Gableran, a specialist from the famous instrument-making Pande clan, is driven to the village all the way from Blahbatuh. He is greeted with coffee and sweets. After some polite chitchat, we escort him to the temple, where he begins tuning the instruments.

Sadia says, "Oh the gods will be easily attracted if the music is sweet."

There is already a lot of concern that the poorly tuned gamelan has offended the gods. Others argue the offerings haven't been quite right. More and more people have headaches. Something is out of kilter in the village, or so some think, which makes everyone apprehensive of the wrath of the gods.

The tuner man shaves the keys, strikes them, and compares the sounds. He adjusts the height of the bamboo under the metal keys until a loud clear sound emerges. He smiles when he finds the "sweet spot." The small crowd "ahhs" and agrees. The gods will certainly be drawn to the sound.

After the tuner leaves, I work with some of the men to erect an impromptu palm ceiling over a section of the temple.

Here offerings will be placed. More twisting of bamboo strips, lacing of the woven mats. It's a natural routine now. I go to and from gamelan practice in the temple, unescorted. I've learned the easiest of two patterns—one for the *Baris*, a warrior dance, and one for the *Topeng*, the masked dance.

In the afternoon, we gather and sift dirt that will be used for the foundation of the house. Eddie shows me a bag of stuff that he's been collecting from the market during our trips to town. There's wire, and cloth, and religious artifacts. He takes out some of his stolen poems, wraps them in cloth, and then, with wire, wraps them around one of the foundation stones.

"Hey, help me. We'll make offerings together," he says excitedly.

"No, Eddie, I want to practice gamelan," I say.

"You're willing to do any ritual with the Balinese, but you won't do any with me! Why is that? Any ritual brings you in touch with god's love."

"No, Eddie, it's just that Balinese rituals are ancient, and yours are...well, experimental."

Cutting me off, he says, "How do you think rituals came to be created in the first place? I'm discovering truths even more ancient than Bali's, that love is the basis for power and creativity."

More and more, Eddie is offended if I don't give him the constant attention he demands. But I can't. I have my own thoughts and things I'm trying to learn. That's the problem. Eddie's all in the moment. He doesn't finish anything he starts, such as learning gamelan. I know Ota's at the bottom of this, encouraging him.

I try to take it slowly, and go deeper and deeper every day. My reality is changing. It's a shame I can only share these discoveries with Eddie, and sometimes Big Swede.

Dear Nicholas,

Betty and Bob are traveling to Singapore. Why don't you meet them there? I understand it's not very far away. Your letters cause me to worry. I hope you are healthy. If you want to come home for a visit. Dad can send you money....

Love, Mother

I feel my old self start to fall away, like a snake's skin, something I don't need anymore. Someday soon, I'll leave the old Nick behind.

We carry more of the dense, black stones for the foundation of the house. They are extremely heavy, but the Balinese can move these large stones as if the rocks weighed nothing. It's weird. Even the kids carry large stones heavier than what I can manage.

Eddie can move them easily too.

He says, "Meditate on love, and the vibration of the magnetic polarities shift. The stones become very light."

Strange. I don't know what he's talking about.

Eddie is down at the stream getting more rocks, when four puffy-faced tourists wander through the village and watch the house being built. I ignore them. I'm very proud. It would be a good thing if more travelers chose to live in villages. Permits or not.

I steal a glance at the tourists. Anna, the Australian anthropologist, is one of them! I start to say something to her, but she look right through me. She doesn't recognize me. She looks away. I look down at my filthy sarong and dirty feet. Have I changed so much? I step back into the shadow. I watch them meander down the path until they are out of sight.

More bamboo arrives, ready to be measured and cut. The priest makes offerings at the shrine near the new house. The bamboo joints are cut to fit, together at the precise angle, then reinforced with lashings. The frame of the house goes up quickly. We climb up into the new rafters, careful to keep our sarongs from falling off. By the end of the day, the house is in place. Lobo and Suweca bring me coffee to celebrate.

Eddie goes into Denpasar. I stay in the village. It's good to be by myself.

Dear Adrian,

...Without egging each other on, Eddie and I would never have gotten this far. Now I'm worried about him. His mind flits from one thing to the other. First trance, now rituals. And he's so thin! Well, actually I've lost weight too.

I'm just trying to live simply, which is very hard. Maybe I've had enough of both Eddie and Bali.

Hey, want to meet me in India in a few months?

I am worn out by the intensity of everything. There's no let up. I blame it on Eddie but also the painters, and the kids, and the people, and the insects, and the heat. It's very intense all the time. I try to keep smiling like Sadia, but I've lost center. I've lost weight. I'm losing it here.

Chapter 19

IT'S TABOO

Tonight is the full moon; an auspicious time for firing bricks and the hearts of young girls.

"Tonight my love charm will obtain its full power," says Eddie. We gather with the painters at the kiln beside the house site. It's filled with moist, clay bricks. The fire underneath is kept burning throughout the night. Occasionally one of the men gets up to rekindle the fire.

Ota appears in the shadows. Eddie jumps to his feet and disappears for about half an hour, then returns. He sits quietly for a few minutes, staring into the glowing kiln.

"I know what I must do," says Eddie quietly. "Enter the realm where the spirits reside <u>before</u> they are reincarnated. I can travel with love energy. It's much faster than the speed of light."

"What are you smoking, Eddie? Can I have some?"

Eddie smiles.

"With love energy, the spirits can be influenced before they incarnate."

"If your father could hear you now! A missionary to the ethereal worlds," I joke. "That's a pretty far-out way to change tourists attitudes."

"Drastic times require drastic means."

I don't think he's kidding.

At dawn, when the fire cools, we check the bricks. They are hard. Success. Sadia arrives with the village priest. He consults the lontars to learn which offerings to place in the foundation of the building.

The *pemangku* wraps some bricks in a white cloth, sprinkles them with holy water, and places them in holes that have been dug for the floor. Sadia says there will be a final purification ritual before the house can be occupied.

I re-read a letter that Eddie brought me. It's from Deke, one of my oldest friends. It brings me down.

Nick in paradise....

Hey, your tapes are really cool... John Cage on steroids... I played them for Santana's drummer. He really dug it. He's going to play it for Carlos. The record companies passed. Sorry, man....

Hey, are you all right? You sound spaced. You smoking Bali weed?

Margo's writing poetry and says "howdy."

Peace, Deke

Lobo comes over for gamelan practice. I'm in no mood. I'll be the teacher for a change. I play a Led Zeppelin riff from "You Need Lovin," for Lobo and Rani. I teach it to them, and they play it back without verve, to humor me. It's obvious they aren't getting into it, so I play the actual song on my tape recorder. It's nothing but noise to them; they can't understand it. I know! I'll turn it up louder. Ha, ha!

In the afternoon, we go to Klungkung for more bamboo. When we return to the village, the roof of the house has been half filled in with thatch that women have been weaving for days.

Heads of the workers poke through holes in the roof. I wave. They smile and wave back. They make a game out of whatever they are doing. I film the painters as they play around in the rafters.

I climb atop to help. I try to tie one of the pieces on. It's not as easy as it looks. Lobo finishes the job for me. The grass roof hangs down around the house on all four sides. It reminds me of the lion-maned Barong. Our shaggy house needs a haircut. Sadia says that comes later.

Sadia and I sit and talk for a few hours. I ask him why we can't move into the house; it's been finished for days. He says that the priests must prepare a ceremony first, but this must be done according to the calendar. Even though weeks have passed, the time is not yet auspicious.

"*Nanti*," he says.

Always nanti. Sadia says the priests argue about the proper time and protocol. Plus, there are bigger problems than when to bless our house. The phenomenon of the headaches persist in the village and no one can explain it.

Tonight it is Halloween in the States. As a kid, it was one our my favorite holidays. I was usually Elvis. Eddie was Zorro. Every day is like Halloween in Bali with music, magic, and masks.

Women have been making offerings for days now. The whole village seems to do little but prepare for temple festivals. They must spend half their lives in religious activities.

As it gets dark, Pierre and Nicole Devaux come to the village to see the temple festival and return our processed film. Pierre gives me two film tins.

"It's quite fantastic, your film."

"He ran his copy on his office projector. The Bali Hai manager loved it," says Nicole.

"Come by sometime and I'll show it to you."

They join us on our porch. Eddie is sullen. Sadia, the perfect host, brings some tea and cookies.

Pierre is still working in Sanur on a growth plan of Bali for The World Bank. The greater the growth, the greater the foreign investment in Bali.

We walk to the temple together. Sadia wraps a saput around Nicole's and Pierre's waists before they enter the temple. There are sure a lot of white faces here. It's very unusual. We speak English more and become less involved with our Balinese friends, who are curious about the visitors we've brought to the temple. We don't introduce them.

Pierre proudly explains that in a few years the island's infrastructure—hotels, roads, water treatment, electrical plants—will be able to handle half a million tourists a year. That's more than fifty times the present number!

Eddie blames Devaux for the ill fate that he sees will befall Bali.

"Can't you see you'll be responsible for pollution, prostitution, disease, and the ultimate loss of this culture? Can you live with that?" challenges Eddie.

A shadow play erupts in one corner of the temple. Devaux's camera is loaded with the last of our film. It's a great performance.

Eddie and Pierre keep up their banter. I can't but help overhear Pierre. He reminds Eddie that tourism is not his idea. "I'm just an observer, not a participant."

"But the plans you recommend will disrupt life here," says Eddie.

Every time I point the camera at the screen, the camera jams. Damn. We may not get another chance to use the camera.

"No," says Pierre smugly, "I am just a consultant, we've already addressed your concerns. New investment will bring new medical facilities. Indonesia is entitled to grow out of its Third World status."

Eddie counters, "It sounds like the Bali version of Disneyland. Kidnap tourists for a few days, pick their wallets, and send them home."

I look over. Nicole watches the puppet play. Sadia and a group of villagers fixate on Devaux's and Eddie's conversation.

Devaux grins, "Funny you should mention Disneyland. They want me to do a feasibility study for their theme park in France."

Eddie retorts, "If you had any integrity at all, you'd be living in a village, and not trying to exploit this culture."

Devaux says, "Exploit. Hardly. We are bringing utilities to the island that will be of real value. Like electricity."

The shadows from the screen flicker across Eddie's face.

"What if you could create electricity anywhere, in every village, without wires? Eliminate coal burning, stop building dangerous nuclear plants, and stop exploiting the Indonesian oil fields. Electricity, like air and water. For free! For everyone!"

"Sure, great," snickers Devaux, "But unless I'm mistaken, no one knows how to do that. Anyway, the ball's already rolling. The government has already approved it. It will help the Balinese. A road into their villages will help them get someone out who is sick."

Devaux draws a map in the dust to demonstrate how well everything has been thought out. Sadia and the others stoop down to see it. Eddie stands.

"Look, the plan is brilliant. It really is. All the tourists will be segregated in South Bali, in Nusa Dua. The rest of Bali remains untouched. Other than day trips by bus, the tourists will be contained in Kuta, Sanur, Nusa Dua, and maybe a little in Ubud."

Ubud? Ubud is the island's interior!

I can't imagine hotels in Kuta or Ubud. I feel slightly sickened and am ashamed by my own desires toward "exploitative cultural behavior"—the film, the tour, the painting exhibition. I keep still. Cast no stones.

A nervous priest clutches Sadia's arm. He's distressed that we didn't make offerings for the camera. Is that why it jammed? We forgot our manners. How stupid!

Sadia give me a disappointed look, raising an eyebrow to the offerings.

"No raise camera more high than offerings," Sadia says.

"Ma'af kan sekali," I apologize.

Eddie and Devaux have forgotten they are at a religious ceremony. Both have come unhinged, trying to protect their own points of view. Sadia, Nicole, and I try to shuttle the disruptive pair out of the temple before they cause more disruption.

Sounding like Nostradamus, Eddie prophesies how the culture will come to an end in our lifetime.

Sadia turns to stone. He says nothing, as Pierre climbs into his jeep and slams the door. What a night! Sadia must be in shock. It must be the first time he's heard anything like this, or seen two Westerners argue. Devaux's plan has reached the village level.

Back on the porch Eddie and I try to comfort Sadia.

"Maybe big development will happen. Maybe not."

"*Saya tidak mengerti*," shaking his head.

Eddie jumps in.

"Let me explain. Bali is a good place for tourists because every time a tourist wants something, a Balinese man will say, 'okay, no problem'." If a tourist wants a car, or electricity, or hot water, or a toilet, someone says 'okay, no problem'." But this attitude of trying to please tourists is dangerous."

Sadia nods. He understands. Eddie continues.

"Tourists don't understand the effect of their desires. Everytime they want something and Bali says 'okay,' then bad things will happen. Already many bad things happen in America because people want too many things. Now these things will happen to Bali too because of tourists: traffic jams all over the island, unbreathable smog-filled air, plastic bags, paper and beer cans polluting the rivers, sewage from the hotels destroying the coral reefs, oil spills killing fish and birds? Is this what you want?!!."

"*Tidak mau! Tidak mau!* But what can we do? We are little people, not have big power," cries Sadia.

"We can do something," I say. Travelers like us and others can learn to be rich by living with less. That's what you do. That's why Bali is so fantastic. People must learn they don't need many things to be happy."

Later, Eddie tries to enlist me in a plan.

"You know that rap to Sadia was pure idealism. You think tourists will automatically want to live like hippies. Do without. Never! Well just see that they'll have to do without. The only solution is to use guerilla tactics."

"Eddie, why can't you just enjoy living here, don't worry so much about tourism. Forget it!

"Because it's irresponsible to do nothing!"

"But you can't change people like Devaux and you certainly can't stop tourism!" I retort.

"Something must be done. This is an undeclared war. Strong measures are necessary. We could kidnap the most influencial people we can — investors, planners, government officials — and make them stay in a village and experience Balinese life."

"Are you nuts?"

"No, they'll have time to think and repent. They'll give up their pampered, destructive lifestyles. We can stamp out this madness."

I laugh.

"Yeah, right."

I put an end to this ridiculous conversation by walking out back to see how our house is coming. Eddie follows. As the sun sets, the house is finished and the workers clean up.

"Magnificent, Eddie. It's finally finished," I say as we walk around the house.

"You've got that right," he says, "it's stillborn."

"What are you talking about?" I reply.

"Can't you see? The house. The priest will never be able to reincarnate this house."

"Sure he will, and after the ceremony we'll move in." He doesn't respond. I pick up a flat stone and scratch an "x" on one side.

"Hey, Eddie, let's flip for who gets the bigger room."

He asserts, "It won't matter anymore. It's all over."

Chapter 20

Bagus Sekali, Saya Dengan Gamelan
IT'S OKAY, I'M WITH THE BAND

The next morning I walk around the rice fields. A dozen kids follow me, jumping and shouting. On the village path into Sideman is a small warung. Ota sits with a Westerner who's captivated by his rap.

"Oh, oh," I think to myself, "he's snared another one."

I sit down beside them. Ota ignores me. He is wearing his "priest get-up." The Westerner is French, maybe thirty. He nods to me politely then turns back to Ota.

Ota is as eccentric as ever with his cane, his smudged and broken tortoise-shell glasses, and his mystical rap. It's the same rap he's been giving to Eddie. The Frenchmen pays for another arak.

"Give everything away?" asks the Frenchman.

"Ya, to get Bali magic you must do this," says Ota.

The Frenchman hangs on every word. Is everyone looking for a guru these days?

Just as I think, 'Ota's a little nuts,' he shifts his position and covertly points his feet in my direction —a kind of a Balinese "screw you."

The Frenchman is wearing an amulet like the one Ota gave Eddie. Could Ota be using magic to bond these foreigners to him? To get them to do his bidding? Is this why Eddie's been acting strangely? If it's a love charm, then where's Eddie's beloved?

I'm afraid Ota is taking advantage of Eddie. I get up and leave, "permisi."

Ota takes another sip from his arak and shifts his feet.

Eddie has gone to Denpasar. He returns with six men who carry stuff to the compound. There's no room in the hut so they pile it up in the pavillion. There's wire, girders, electrical components, meters, switches, dynamos, magnets, lots of unrecognizable parts, and more religious paraphernalia.

"Eddie, what is all this stuff?" I ask.

"My generator, it's for my generator, isn't it great?!" he says excitedly, as he inventories the many boxes.

"But where did you get all this?"

Eddie is startled. "Oh, someone gave it to me. They believe in my idea."

"The generator?" I shake my head.

"Listen, it's the greatest idea I've ever had. This generator is a big one. I can produce electricity!"

"You got the idea from Devaux, your arch enemy. And now you've got to prove him wrong. Unbelievable!"

"Hey, so what? Bali doesn't need The World Bank for power. They have me!"

"You're nuts. You don't know the first thing about electricity. Bali's never going to see electricity from that thing."

"I'm learning. Soon the boys here won't have to prostitute their art to get roads and electricity."

Eddie spends the rest of the afternoon and late into the night fooling around with his electrical stuff. Unless there's divine intervention, he's never going to be able to make electricity from this scrap heap.

Tonight is my first Topeng performance with the gamelan in a temple ceremony. All day I am anxious about it. Maybe that's why I spend half the day in Denpasar—I don't want to hang around the village with my nervousness on display.

It's no accident when a copy of Carl Jung's *Symbols of Transformation* arrives at Poste Restante. Nothing yet from the Art Center. There is a brief note from Sonny.

Dear Nicholas,

I dreamt you were looking for a sacred plant. You climbed a mountain from where you could see the whole world.

Love, Sonny

As cryptic as it is, it feels good that Sonny understands what I am going through.

It's late afternoon when I go to "Tom Sawyer's swimming hole." No one is around. I take off my clothes and float in the shallow, cool, moving waters. I close my eyes. I drift off.

I feel something move beside me. I open my eyes and see a large carp disappear in the dark currents. I close my eyes and again feel something or someone's presence. I open my eyes slowly but they are gently covered by warm fingers. I think it's *her.*

She massages my tight neck, and then my arms and chest. I feel the tension dissipate. I try to look again and she covers my face with her palm. She bends over me. I feel her breast as she moves down to massage my thighs, calves, and feet. No, not a massage, a kind of energy transfer.

The energy circles up to my forehead, then stops at the crown of my head. I wait for a moment and listen. I only hear the water rushing past. I open my eyes and she is gone. Was she really here? I dress, alert and clearheaded. I'm ready.

In the hut, I prepare my best shirt. (I have only two.) Lobo helps me dress. I put on a *saput* and a *kein* (a large piece of cloth which hangs from the waist to the knees) over my sarong. It's all I can do to get everything to stay up. Lobo makes subtle adjustments in the knots. He hands me a headband with a metallic golden flower. Yes! He lends me a turquoise cotton jacket like all the players wear. Cool. He puts a kris in the *kein.* The final touch. I feel high as we walk to the temple. I can barely feel my feet on the ground, I'm so excited. This is going to be great.

Eddie watches as I get ready.

"This is your chance," Eddie says. "An invitation to trance. Go for it. Enter the world of the gods, and serve them."

"You mean, break a leg?" I say, as I leave the compound. Eddie laughs.

The gamelan instruments are no longer in the pavilion. They're set out in the main courtyard. The pavilion is being used for dancers who are gossiping and getting dressed.

Lobo says, "you sit here" and then walks off.

Beside me is Agus, a white-haired, older man; one of the dancers from Padangtunggal. That explains why I haven't seen him before. He asks for a kretek, and lights it. He then asks for a second kretek which he puts in his pocket for *nanti* (later). Coffees and cookies are served to the visitors, as is the custom. No one seems in much of a rush about anything. (Five minutes to show time, Nipas!)

Lobo returns and leads me to a mat. He sits behind one of the instruments. I sit behind him. People are milling about. In a large open space, a makeshift doorway with a curtain has been improvised. Behind the curtain is a bamboo room. This is where the Topeng dancers will emerge and return to change costumes and masks before reappearing as different characters.

I wonder if someone will tell me when the piece I know will be played. Without warning, wooden mallets strike the golden keys as the gamelan explodes with a furious volley of notes. De-li-li-li-li-li-de... BAM...BAM....GONG!!

The pace is frenzied. But the musicians sit coolly, their hands a blur. Serious attitude. They gaze off, almost as if they aren't here. The sound is deafening. The smoke from dangling kreteks caresses their cheeks in the still air.

They play effortlessly at lightning speed. Eddie laughs with Ota at one of his own jokes. Villagers gather around the open space, pushing in slightly on the performance area. Everyone is very casual and relaxed. Everyone, that is, except me.

Celestial beauties laden with offerings of fruit sway into line, as the procession enters the adjoining courtyard. It's a brief apparition, and then they are gone. Incredible.

The gamelan stops as quickly as it began, and the low gong rings off in the air. A few conversations can be heard.

Dogs bark near the front of the temple. The musicians shift slightly, and some move to other instruments. The priest's raspy incantations can be heard from over the next wall in the temple. I smell the sweet incense.

No one has told me what to do or when to do it. I am very nervous. Am I supposed to play or what? When? More people crowd through the temple gates. Wait, wait.

Chapter 21

Silakan Sanghyang
INVITATION TO TRANCE

"Tonight, you meet Cululuk," says Lobo, poking me in the ribs with his mallet. He gestures toward a vacated instrument that awaits me. It's the metallaphone on which I've been practicing. My axe.

A solo player begins just as I get into position. I wipe my sweaty palm so I don't lose the *panggul.* The drummer catches my eye and WHAP... everyone comes in together. Except me. My first strike is tentative. (Hey, we didn't rehearse this fast!) After a few repetitions, I've got it. With each cycle of the pattern, I gain a little more confidence. Just then the tempo abruptly doubles, and I drop a beat. I struggle to catch the rhythm again.

The curtain is parted by blood-red fingernails. A huge female monster comes out. She looks like Rangda's maidservant. She must be Cululuk. She moves seductively in a circle. Her long tongue hangs down between bulbous breasts over a sagging belly. She bellows, then licks her long fingernails.

"Anak anak, enak enak!" she bellows. (Children, children, delicious, delicious!)

I look back down to keep up with the rapid changes, then up again, so I won't miss Cululuk's action.

She spies a tasty child to pluck from the audience to quench her ravenous hunger. The adults press in around the dance area. In the front, terrified youngsters are boxed in by laughing adults behind. There is no escape. The adolescents are only a little less fearful than their younger siblings. They think their younger brothers' and sisters' fear is funny, until the monster looks their way.

The hideous monster paces slowly, dangerously, around the dusty circle, making her final decision from the most delectable children. (I am finally in the groove with the music and relax enough to watch.) Hey, this is fun, until...

The she-monster looks at Eddie, then directly at me and points accusingly. (Hey, you've got the wrong guy!) No big deal, she'll look away. She wants a child...doesn't she? But no, she keeps staring. It's me she wants!

"Hey, I'm with the band," I plead, "you couldn't want me." Tension builds as the filthy creature drags her body near, 30 feet away, now 20, now 10. Her bulbous, penetrating eyes, lascivious tongue, decaying body. Ugh!

The gamelan beats steadily. I keep in the groove. It plays me. I can't look away. I am becoming lost. Hypnotized. The hallucinations begin. The she-monster is dangerously near. It's me she wants. The gamelan pulls to a quick false stop, as I duck her blow. She comes at me again. I restrain her by grabbing her necklace with one hand. With the other, I raise my kris to stab her in the chest, but am repelled backwards.

I fall hard on my back. Now she charges. I raise my kris again, but it turns in on my chest. I return to consciousness. My instrument rings out in the pause. The audience cheers and laughs. What's going on here?

The gamelan kicks back in and picks up the pace—sprinting. We have never played this fast. Come on guys, slow down! My arms begin to cramp. I look up at the she-monster. She leans over me. Her furry breasts and necklace of entrails dangle in my face. She smells like rotting food. I don't know whether I am playing or not. Sweat rolls down my face. Mocking, the monster wipes her brow. The crowd howls as the demon spins on her heels and heads in another direction. I am spared!

She grabs an inattentive child who screams in terror, as she is raised above the monster's head and open mouth. The she-monster thrashes her feet in a frenzied dance. The crowd loves it. I glance at Lobo. He's doubled over with laughter. The other musicians are all cracking up. It's all they can do to hold it together. My initiation to the gamelan. At least I wasn't eaten. I'm dazed, disoriented. Lobo drags me off the instrument. Huh? Holy moly, what happened here? I'm confused.

I sit on the mat as the next piece begins. Consciousness returns. I feel better. And better. And great, really great. I just played in a temple ceremony with a Balinese gamelan!

Eddie comes up. He's thrilled.

"You found the gateway in. I knew you could do it. Now maybe you'll understand what I'm trying to do and quit fighting me."

After the ceremony, I sit with Agus who pulls the second "for later" kretek out of his pocket and lights it. The musicians hang out, smoke, and move the instruments back inside the pavilion. Then Agus gently picks up the basket which contains the now harmless she-monster costume. He winks and wanders off into the darkness toward his village. Are you kidding me? That little old man was Cululuk?!!

Chapter 22

PAYBACK

The roosters announce dawn. I wake with a premonition that something awaits me in Denpasar. Eddie and I leave early. Sure enough, there is a large envelope. Inside are three reviews of the Balinese painting exhibition at the San Francisco Art Center. There's also an international money order for $6,000 for paintings sold. I go to the bank and cash it.

"All right!" shouts Eddie, as he gives me the closed-fist "power sign."

On the way back to the village, I calculate that $6,000 is half the annual income for the whole village! Since I'm down to my last $100, I split the wad of rupiah notes in half and figure $3,000 is my just share. No, that's too much. Maybe I should keep 10 percent, like an agent. I keep $600.

The whole bemo ride consists of me shifting money back and forth—more to the village, and then more to me. I'm about to drive myself crazy. I need the money, but so do they. Look at all they've done for me, and all I've done in return is to buy coffee or kreteks. I see what Wayan Linah means about my "monkey mind."

We get out of the bemo and walk down the path towards "Tom Sawyer's swimmin' hole."

"Why do you keep shifting all our money around?" asks Eddie.

"I'm trying to decide how much to keep and how much to give Sadia," I answer. "Just split it, fifty-fifty," he decides.

"What do you mean fifty-fifty?" I say. "Give Sadia half? They deserve more."

Eddie says, "No, no, no, give me half. It was my idea. I get half."

"What?!! It wasn't your idea!" I protest. "You weren't even around when I planned the show with Sadia."

"But they'll just make more paintings," Eddie says. "I need more money for something from which everyone will benefit. My generator. A big one. If we can produce electricity. Bali won't need The World Bank!"

I say, "You're nuts. You don't know what you're talking about."

He says, "I'm learning. You can give me my share of the money right now and I'll show you what I can do."

"No, the money's going to Sadia. Sadia can do what he wants with his share."

Eddie says, "Why give them a fish when you can teach them to fish?"

Eddie goes off and sits by the stream and sulks. I take a mandi, meditate, and try to calm my mind.

Sadia is working on a painting when I arrive. How unusual. It's the first time I've seen him paint with the group.

He looks up, beaming. Does he know about the money? That smile. Of course he does! I empty one pocket and then the next. Two giant rolls of rupiah notes. He puts his hands together.

"Om Shanti Shanti, Nipas," he says.

By midafternoon, there are twice the number of painters on the porch and lots of new colors. They are painting up a storm, singing and laughing. I get lots of appreciative looks. I feel proud that I am able to do something for them at last.

Eddie grabs a canvas and some paints and pushes his way into the corner. The other painters back away and give him room. He works furiously for a few hours, his back against the corner, not letting anyone see. His energy is dark. I go over to him.

He rises and says, "You don't want electricity, you don't want miracles, you want paintings. Here's what you want..."

With this, he disdainfully tosses it on the ground. The painters gather around, dumbfounded.

There is no structure. Only chaos. Everywhere are fragmented body parts: anuses, breasts, penises, nostrils. Orifice shapes, carelessly rendered, smeared, thrown onto the page in contempt. Lightning bolts shooting through everything. Decapitations, arms, legs, plants, houses, temples, tourist buses, dogs. Everything pulled apart and thrown over a murky jungle landscape. The painters view the work and quietly leave. Afraid. Eddie seems proud of this work which insults the gods and terrifies the rest of us.

Big Swede visits the village. He too can senses that Eddie is under Ota's spell. When Ota is not giving Eddie a lesson in metaphysics, they are drinking buddies tossing down cup after cup of arak.

I share my frustrations with Swede.

"I think Eddie's in trouble. His energy is very dark."

Big Swede is aloof, not about to get involved. "It's all *maya*, man. You can't do anything. Just play it out. That's your karma."

Morning. Eddie is gone. Lobo tells me he left a few hours earlier. Probably went into Denpasar. I go for long walk in the surrounding *sawahs.* I help some farmers wash their cows in the stream. Later I sit at a warung, have some lunch, then meander into Padangtunggal, a nearby village.

By chance I meet Agus, the white-haired, old man who danced Cululuk at my gamelan performance. We laugh about that night. He invites me to his house and courtyard, which is filled with every variety of red-and-green parrot.

He's very interested in how I like living in the village. I tell him it's been the greatest thing I've ever done and that we have just finished building a house, but have not moved into it yet.

I don't fully understand but he says something about my shakti, my power being increased because Cululuk came to the ceremony. Whatever it is, it makes me feel good.

Night falls quickly. I find my way back to the village by flashlight. Not fun. I don't like wandering around deserted rice fields at night.

Outside the village I see a red light. It looks far away. Suddenly I realize it's close. A cigarette ember? It moves. I shine the flashlight on Eddie's face. His lips are smeared with blood-red juices from chewing betel nut.

"Jeez, Eddie, you scared the hell out of me. What are you doing out here?"

He's so excited he can't talk. He motions for me to follow him.

"I did it. I finally did it."

"What are you talking about, Eddie?"

"You'll see."

He's all worked up. Scary. He leads me behind the village to Ota's compound. We go behind the hut.

"What...?"

"Quiet," he whispers. He slowly pulls back a flap on the back wall of the hut. I peer through the slats. A small oil lamp illuminates the room. The Devauxs are tied up and blindfolded! Ota performs some ritual as he watches over them.

I pull Eddie back outside the compound.

"Jesus Christ, Eddie!! What the hell are you doing?"

"I did it! I did it!"

"You did it, all right!! You kidnapped them!!"

"Yes! Yes! It was great. With my Rangda mask and kris."

"What Rangda mask?"

"You know... the one from Kuta."

"Jesus, Eddie. Have you gone mad? You want to get yourself killed? Oh no, what are we going to do?!!"

"We're going to keep them. Show them real village life. And then let them go."

"Eddie, let them go now. Devaux doesn't have the power to stop tourism..."

"Yes, he does. The government listens to him."

"No, no, no. Tourism is coming with or without him. You've got to let them go."

"Let them go? Let them go? There's a war going on. The Balinese are being invaded. We'll kidnap other tourists. Bad publicity will stop tourism just like that!"

"No, what will happen is you'll be arrested."

"It'll be worth it."

"You can't take on tourism by yourself."

"Don't you see? Once they learn how great the village is,

they'll understand that they've been brainwashed. Like we'd been brainwashed."

"Eddie, I can't go along with this. You've got to let them go."

"No way. We're going to stick to our plan."

I've never seen Eddie so intense. So resolute. How do I get Pierre and Nicole back without getting caught? Eddie is not going to quit so easily.

"Kidnapping people is the slow way. You've got the right concept but the wrong method, " I try to trick him.

"Let's film the Devauxs all tied up—with Pierre's own camera!—and send the footage to the news stations with a press release about how tourists all over Bali are being kidnapped." Eddie lights up. He loves the idea of using Devaux's camera.

Eddie plays some gamelan tapes to cover the sound of the camera, as I shoot footage of them.

Once this is done, we borrow Ota's son's bemo and load the blindfolded Devauxs in the back. Eddie sits beside them wearing the Rangda mask, and commands them in Indonesian. I am terrified he's going to say something in English and be recognized.

I get into the front seat and drive us to Sanur. How'd I get into this? What am I going to do? I can barely drive, I shake so. The dark side of the dream is emerging.

I stop on a path a few blocks from the Bali Hai Hotel. I get out and unload the Devauxs. When I untie Nicole, her hand accidentally touches my ring.

("That's okay. Lots of people have rings," I tell myself.)

On the way back, Eddie is high from the kidnapping.

"It worked, it really worked!"

Eddie threatens to kidnap more tourists unless I promise to help him start his generator in two days, before the full moon "when it will be the most effective."

"Sure, Eddie, sure, I promise." Anything so he won't pull another stunt which could end our life in Bali.

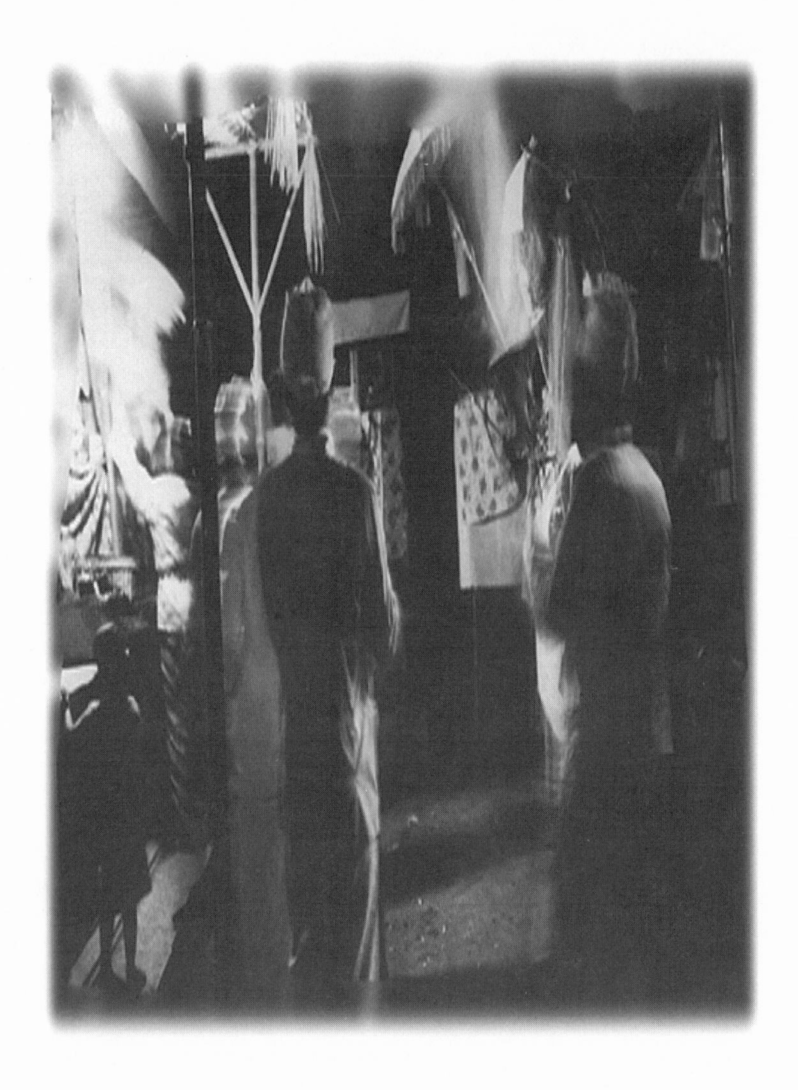

Chapter 23

Melaspas
OFFERINGS

The house is ready for its next incarnation. The priest arrives and begins *melaspas,* a purification ritual that will bring the house to life. He lays out small pieces of the house—bamboo, grass, earth, stones. Everything that was killed and now has to be reincarnated. Then the house will be a living thing with feet, a body, and a head. He arranges the offerings, incense and holy water, and begins chanting.

About halfway through, he gets ups. Sadia rushes over. They talk for a moment or two, then the priest leaves. Sadia looks flushed but continues to smile.

"Something wrong, I don't know. Maybe try again. Maybe wrong day. I don't know."

It's ironic. We're just about to move into the house and now the ceremony backfires, and Eddie is freaking out on me. Maybe the house is "dead." And we're dead if Pierre figures out who kidnapped him. Will Nicole remember the ring? We could be arrested anytime. What a mess.

At lunch, another *drama makan*, Eddie takes a handful of rice, chews it for a moment, then spits it on a leaf palm. He repeats this process until he has a sticky mound of rice. From this "original soil," he begins to "create the world" and makes little rice figures. He holds them in each hand and makes them dance. Sadia and the other painters watch in disbelief.

"I'm making an offering for the house," he says, a bit hurt.

Now Eddie carries on about a plan to import wild ponies from Australia.

"This way we can ride from village to village," he says. "We won't need to build roads or drive polluting bemos. And, my Balinese princess will ride behind me. Hah!"

Good. Maybe this will occupy his mind and he'll forget that I promised to help him with his generator tomorrow because the "moon will be right." I can't take all this.

I've got to go off by myself. A pack of kids follows me. I turn around and tell them I want to be alone, but there is no way to say it in Indonesian. There is no concept for being alone. This is one of the most densely populated areas of the world, so "alone" has no meaning. I keep repeating *sendiri*, which means "one," but the kids are baffled. I tell them to "stay," but when I turn my back, like puppies, they've shuffled a few feet closer. When I walk, they follow. I reach the stream and bathe. The kids stop on the overlooking hillside and watch.

I get in the stream. The cool water calms me down. I close my eyes and remember how I got here and why.

A year ago, I had no desire whatsoever to travel to the Far East or Southeast Asia. Sure, I liked the Eastern sensibility. I could have gone to Canada, but an internal compass brought me to the East. I was looking for something.

I was seeking pure experience. I threw myself into a culture to see if I could survive. I wanted to find the commonalties among people. I wanted to take a hard look at my own life. I had to find out who I am and what is important to me.

I told myself I would never go back to America. Its comforts and conveniences keep you out of touch with yourself and nature. America was crashing and burning. I had to find a new life.

Marshall MacLuhan gave me the idea. Maybe I could live as a "global citizen." Bucky Fuller pointed out that when you look at the photos of earth that the astronauts brought back, you don't see any boundaries between countries. As a global citizen, I am entitled to travel anywhere. It would be a grand experiment. Dirty was okay. Sleeping on the ground was okay.

The air-conditioned, power-steering, self-defrosting, self-cleaning-oven mentality of the West is death. Give me texture, sensation, gritty reality. Let it be chaotic, very loud, or very quiet. Fill it with strange smells and sensations. Let me try everything. And here I am. I got what I ordered.

The bath clears my head. I need more time to think. I need a break from the kids, from the painters, from the village, and from Eddie.

The house is finished. Maybe I'll make offerings for the house. I'll go to Gunung Agung, the volcano and home of the gods. Sadia thinks it's a great idea. He says this will please the gods and help the priests to reincarnate the house. He gives me a prayer to memorize and say with my offerings.

Om Shanti Shanti.

I bow my head and
hold high these hands
with your offerings of
foods and flowers with sweet perfumes
so that you may be pleased.

I ask for new life,
and shall daily give thanks
for your gifts and kindness:
for your bamboo and grass and stone
so within your house I may rest.

Om Suasti Asti.

Chapter 24

Gunung Agung
THE VOLCANO

I quietly climb out of the bamboo bed, trying not to make any noise. As I step on the floor, it creaks. Eddie bounces in, a sarong around his waist. He is full of energy.

"Where ya going? Denpasar? I'll go with you."

"Gunung Agung."

"The volcano? How come?"

"To make offerings."

"But Nick, what about the generator? You promised."

I put on my Levi's and zip them up.

"I only promised so that you'd shut up about it. I saved your butt the other night, Eddie. I didn't come here to save your butt."

"But Nick, the kidnapping worked. Together we can keep Bali from being exploited. Generate free electricity. I just need your help..."

"Eddie, I don't care about your plans. Your plans to build a generator are crap! All your ideas are crap! Nobody cares, Eddie. Not me, not the painters, not Sadia. Nobody wants to hear any more about your damned generator...except maybe Ota and he's whacked as well."

I put on my plastic sandals.

"Ota believes it will work. Come with me to Denpasar. I need some more wire, some metal rods... Wait a sec."

Eddie goes into the other room. Exasperated, I continue dressing. Eddie returns wearing a t-shirt. He holds two of his rice sculpture people and moves them about strangely. Now what's he doing?

"It is <u>our</u> house. I should pray too."

"Fine. You and Ota make offerings."

"No, you're right, we'll pray on Gunung Agung—together. I'm ready to go!"

I put an extra shirt in my shoulder bag, grab an orange, toss it in and rise. Eddie blocks the doorway.

"Here, take this," he insists, as he holds out a rice sculpture person. "For the offering."

"Get out of the way, Eddie! I don't want your stinking doll!"

Eddie points at my sandals.

"Are you going to climb the mountain in those sandals?"

"What?!!" I turn, kick off the sandals, reach under the bed for my boots, and put them on. I turn around as Eddie steps back in the doorway, holding a rice sculpture person. I push past him.

"See ya."

Eddie follows me out of the hut and down the path to the compound gate.

Eddie watches, clutching the rice-sculpture person as if he were a child about to cry. Then I turn and walk down the path out of the village. I hear Eddie behind me.

"Nick?!"

I keep walking.

The volcano looms up in the distance maybe 10 or 20 kilometers away. I've got plenty energy. I'll walk. I follow a narrow path into the rice fields.

I am glad to be away from Eddie. I need to think. Moving into the house doesn't feel right. This pilgrimage to Gunung Agung is what a Balinese would do.

The volcano is big, really big. Walking through the rice fields takes longer than I thought. The volcano is still pretty far away and in less than an hour, it gets dark. I need to find someplace to stay.

Few foreigners ever visit this side of the island. Every few minutes along the way people stop me.

"Dari mana? Kemana?" they ask.

"*Saya dari Sindu. Desa saya. Saya pergi ke Gunung Agung, untuk berdoa. Rumah baru saya sudah habis.*" ("I'm from Sindu. My village. I am on my way to Gunung Agung, to pray. My new house is finished.") They appreciate my respect for Balinese custom. I feel like a pilgrim.

It's night. I keep walking. The moon is almost full, so it is easy to see my way. In the distance, I hear the clanks from an out-of-tune gamelan. I walk toward the sound.

In a small compound, half a dozen boys, aged nine or ten, play the same Topeng piece that I know. Synchronicity. In a corner, shaving a bronze key, is an old man. One *gangsa* is free—as if waiting for me. The small group continues to play. The old man looks up for a moment. I nod to the empty instrument. The old man nods back. I go over and sit behind it and begin playing with the next repetition. We play faster and faster. The group is young and inexperienced. I fit right in. We finish the piece, and then I excuse myself, "Permisi."

The old man nods. No big deal. I leave as they begin another piece. No one waves; no crowd forms. I am an outsider, but I am treated like one of them.

I walk on. Suddenly I am very tired. A man along the path asks where I am going. I tell him that I need a place to sleep. He takes me a short distance to a tiny one-room house. He calls out to his friends nearby who join us. Once again, it's *drama makan*, and I am the local entertainment. He makes coffee. I talk about California and other places. Hours pass. I am so tired. I ask and am granted permission to sleep.

The next morning, I wake, eat some bananas, drink coffee, and thank my host. I start walking toward the volcano. The day begins sunny, but soon it becomes overcast. If there's any time to take this old tab of acid that I've been carrying around for a year, it's now. It's probably no good anyway.

By afternoon I am at the base of Gunung Agung, and it looks like rain. The walk took far longer than I thought. The volcano is a massive looming mountain in front of me. There is a narrow path leading up. Trees, bushes, and undergrowth extend from either side of the old, black-lava river, crust from previous eruptions.

It begins to rain; first lightly, then heavily. I am sorry that I didn't bring a poncho (not that I had one). Around my waist is an extra shirt; I put it on over my first. This is more symbolic than practical. In a few minutes, I am completely soaked. Every so often, I stop for shelter among clusters of small trees. It doesn't help. The only food I have is the orange. I plan to save it until I am unbearably hungry.

Hours pass. I've climbed up a thousand feet. Below, villages, jungles, and rice fields fan out in a 180 degree panorama. Faraway, near the shore, is a reflection. It's from the Bali Hai Hotel. Beyond is the ocean.

When the rain lets up, I continue. It is very quiet. I haven't seen anyone since the beginning of the ascent. I follow the path, what little there is of it.

Is that music? No, it can't be. A choral group. Gregorian chants. Are these sounds coming from inside my head? Then desires begin surfacing. I want a milkshake. No, I crave a milkshake! Now I want a woman. I laugh.

Suddenly, I feel this heavy weight on my chest. I have this feeling that the world has altered. My life will never be the same again. My jaw tightens. There is a metallic taste in my mouth. I feel stronger. I keep asking myself the same question over and over: "Have-I-done-everything-I-came-here-to-do?" It becomes a chant. Then, as Eddie might do, I alter the words with each repetition.

Have I done everything I came here to do?
Have I felt everything I came here to feel?
Have I thought everything I came here to think?
Have I learned everything I came here to learn?
Have I become everything I came here to be?

Over and over. The images of my life in Bali fold over themselves. I feel the answer is "yes." The thoughts slow down. The moments between the thoughts stretch out. A quiet void. I am breathing heavily. There is no time to think, only to do.

The hiking becomes more strenuous. The incline is even greater. I'm about halfway up the side of the volcano. I come to a primitive stone altar in a small clearing. The gods are drawn to flowers, so I pick some wild ones and fold fresh leaves together. My own version of an offering doesn't look half as good as the ones the village women make.

I kneel and put my hands together in a Balinese mudra. I thank the gods for our new house, my new friends, my health, and for the good fortune of being in Bali. I thank the gods for the music, and the opportunity to learn. I pray for Eddie, for my family and friends back home. I meditate for about twenty minutes, but my body shivers in these wet clothes.

It's late. There's only about another half-hour of sunlight left. It's still raining lightly. I have to decide. Should I return or continue? Sadia had told me to go to the stone altar where the Balinese pilgrims leave their offerings and then return. I've reached my goal, yet another part of me wants to go on, filled with the momentum of climbing. The energy has built up and, as Eddie would say, "I can't help myself."

Without knowing why, I start climbing again. About half an hour later, I remember that I forgot to say the prayer that Sadia had given me.

Climbing higher is foolish. Humans have no business being on the volcano where the gods live. But the impulsive, obsessive, masculine side of me demands I keep going. It's late, and I'm very hungry.

The sun gives a final burst as it drops behind the horizon, yielding the night sky to the moon and low clouds. The climbing is even steeper over the loose volcanic ash and sharp rocks. Nothing holds. I climb a few feet then slide back in a mini-avalanche. A stick becomes my cane. I grab onto roots of small bushes and pull myself up. I'm crawling more than walking. My pounding heart is audible outside my body.

The moonlight casts long shadows on the lava. There is no vegetation. I feel like I'm on Mars. I slip and slide in the loose rocks, starting larger avalanches behind me. I push and pull myself up with my cane. My boots are torn and scraped. When I stop to empty them of the sharp rocks, my feet are swollen and numb.

Hours pass. Unthinking, like an animal driven by instinct, I keep moving, always up. I am driven, obsessed with "conquering the mountain." My body wants to stop, but I want to keep going. I'm gasping to catch my breath. My heart is pumping dangerously fast. I look behind me. The moonlight casts eerie shadows on the swiftly moving clouds below. The wind picks up. It's cold. The lights of the villages spread out like twinkling fireflies all the way to the sea. This is another planet. The moon is reflected in the sea. My consciousness is free to go anywhere.

Looking into the bright reflection on the ocean, then away into the darkness, I see images of the village. Our newly constructed house is illuminated by the moon. Someone is moving inside. It is Eddie. He is naked and rubbing dirt from the foundation stones all over his body. A row of tiny rice-people sculptures sit in witness. He digs a hole in the middle of the house floor. My mind's eye takes me closer. He carefully places two coconut bowls filled with water in the hole and gently drops in flower petals. The bowls are connected by wire, bamboo, and pieces of torn paper. He tears another picture of a mountain lion and a hawk from the "National Geographic," puts them in a broken pot which he ties to his stomach, then climbs, like a pregnant monkey, into the rafters of the house. Eddie takes a large bamboo pole and, using it like a telescope, views the moon. A metal rod is attached to the end of the bamboo pole like an antennae. Then he pans the bamboo spy glass until he sees Ota, who nods approvingly from the shadows below. Eddie waves the bamboo pole like a wand and shouts.

I shiver and lose the waking dream. My hands are cut from many falls. It doesn't matter; I feel nothing. I am no longer hungry. I just want to make it to the top.

By midnight, I am crawling on all fours. If I stand, I'm afraid I'll fall. My feet are too weak to walk. My jeans are torn at the knees. Only a few hundred feet more to the top. A seventy-degree angle. I pull myself up with my hands. Only a few more yards! Only a few more feet! I am almost at the top. I am almost a god!

This can't be! The volcano has tricked me. This isn't the top!

The angle of incline had been so great that I couldn't see that the *actual* top is still a few hundred feet away. And between where I am and the top is a fifteen-foot crevice. Maybe I could jump? No, it's too far. Not with these ruined legs. I crawl along the edge of the crevice trying to find a shorter distance across. It's too far. If I miss, I'll fall thousands of feet. My feet wobble—I have climbed for eighteen hours. Ten thousand feet above Bali. I realize I'll never make it to the very top. My heart is pounding. Damn! Now what?

A gust of wind sends a chill across my chest and brings me to my senses. I need to eat. I need to sleep. I dig a nook under a boulder and crawl in like a wounded animal. I am shivering. I put my freezing hands in my shoulder bag and feel something.

I pull out one of Eddie's rice-people sculptures. He must have sneaked it into the bag somehow.

"It'll be a rice person that saves me," I shout. "Hah!"

I am so hungry that I munch down the whole thing. This only makes me more aware of how hungry I am. I find and eat the orange. I'm starving!

My body aches against the sharp stones, as feeling returns. My legs are beginning to cramp. I can't stay here. I'll freeze. I'm going to have to get off the volcano.

My stick helped me up, but descending is another matter. The lava stones are very loose, and landslides start easily. I have to be careful. The most effective way is to "surf" or "ski" down, a stretch at a time. I slide on both feet for 10 yards or so until I lose my balance, then I fall on my butt to stop. I'm not going to last long this way. I experiment with less painful ways of descending. None works very well. Each fall knocks the breath out of me.

With the moon now at my back, my shadow is directly in front of me. A stumbling shadow puppet in the lead role. A gamelan in my head accompanies my falls. I am being ridiculed by my own mind. The gods are cruel, but then I have no business being on their mountain. I forgot to say the prayer.

Lava dust whips up, blinding me, scratching my eyes. I plunge again into the rocks. Another painfully slow hour. Clumps of vegetation then appear, giving me the hope that the ground will hold. But when I prod the growth with my cane, it gives way to more landslides. A deep ravine—an infinite pit—becomes visible just a few feet to my right. Got to be careful.

The wind rips suddenly as I take my next step, knocking me off balance. I push my cane forward, as another gust swats me from behind like a giant hand. My legs give way and I tumble head over heels in midair into the ravine. I brace myself to crash to the ground, but I don't.

I keep falling and falling.

Time slows down. A flood of thoughts flash through my mind—I feel so foolish and arrogant—"conquering" the volcano. I pick up speed in the fall. Any moment, the fatal wallop.

Instead, I'm caught like a baseball in a giant glove made of branches. I land upside down in the yoke of a fir tree. The boughs bounce from my weight. Upside down, I watch the moon jiggle as the boughs thrash about wildly. Insane, hysterical laughter echoes off the ravine walls. Curious, I think. It stops when I realize the laughter is mine. Time has stopped. It's as if a god knocked me off the volcano with a left hand, then caught me with the right.

Humbly, I climb out of the tree and say a prayer of thanks. My shoulders are smashed and bruised, but nothing seems broken. I must be in shock, adrenaline pumping.

I am lost. I can't climb back up to the path—it's hundreds of feet above me. I find another cane stick and continue my descent. I'm glad to be alive. There are many more clumps of vegetation, all dangerous. Some hold. Some don't and give way. First I twist my ankle. Then an arm. No matter how much I test before each step, I still fall. The volcano is beating me to a pulp. It's not over.

Hours later, I am totally exhausted, battered, and still lost. I have to go on if I am to live.

"Why didn't I say the prayer? I should say it now!" The din of animal and insect sounds increases when I stop walking. I say the prayer aloud to the spirits of the small trees and large vines all around me.

The moon is on the other side of the volcano. It is very dark. I wonder if there are any komodo dragons on Bali. I poke loudly to scare any unwelcome creatures away. I trip and fall.

Ahead, luminous moths are beating their wings, flying in small circles.

When I follow them, I don't seem to fall. Am I imagining this? I test my theory. If the moths change direction, I do. Sure enough. If I follow them, I can walk without falling. The luminous moths lead me off the volcano!

At dawn, the moths vanish and I am deep in a forest. I slide down a small ravine on my back and into a shallow stream. I rest for a moment before drinking thirstily.

In my mind's eye, I see Eddie lying under the pavilion. Ota is chanting and walking around him. Eddie's arms are outstretched. Ota is encouraging Eddie to go deeper. Guiding him. Eddie moves his arm. It lands on a chicken at the same time that there is a clap of lightning and thunder. It is as if he found the switch to the universe's power center and turned it on.

A clap of lightning and thunder in the distance. I wash my arms and hands, which are covered with blood and ash. My head pounds from hunger. My legs shake. I am not sure I can stand again. I have to keep going.

But which direction? I am lost in dense undergrowth. The terrain is nearly flat, and now it is difficult to tell which way to go. I hear something. It stops. I move. It moves. Ahead, about 30 yards, a small girl peeks out from behind a palm. Then she hides. I shout to her, but my voice is dry and doesn't work. I hobble in her direction. She appears ahead of me. I follow.

She lets me glimpse her more often now; she's about seven years old. Is she curious? Where is she going? She carries a red plastic bucket. Are there others nearby? I come upon a path and follow it to a clearing. Then she disappears.

Nearby, is a dilapidated bamboo hut. It looks abandoned until a tiny farmer comes out. I don't want to frighten him. Too late. I collapse in front of his hut.

From his meager garden of some twenty stalks of corn, he picks two large ears. He looks at me and picks another, then roasts them over coals. I begin eating immediately, without waiting for them to even cool off. It is the best corn I've ever tasted! He pours boiling water over coffee grounds. My strength returns as I drink.

After an hour's rest, I thank him for the food, remove my outer shirt, and present it ceremoniously as a gift. It's all

I have. I am so grateful. The shirt is dirty, torn, and still wet, but he doesn't mind. He smiles and thanks me profusely! He bows and points me in the direction of the path back to Sindu.

Chapter 25

Pulang Ke Sindu
THE RETURN

Around 6:00 A.M., I cross a stream. I am really filthy. I wash off. My boots are completely shredded from the lava. My feet are bloody. I feel like I have run a marathon. I buy some fruit from a warung when it opens, then sit down under a tree. I fall into a dream within moments.

There is Eddie in a double-exposure photograph. One of the faces comes alive and begins tearing pages out of a book. Then he takes off all his clothes and methodically puts his shirt and pants on backwards. He runs backwards to a white horse and rides it backwards until he comes to a clearing. Here he dismounts backwards and walks backwards into a large puddle. He bathes in the puddle and becomes nearly black with mud. A large palm frond appears in one hand, a coconut shell in the other. Standing under a waterfall, he sings into the shell with the raspy voice of a dalang and waves the frond like the kayon puppet (tree of life). A woman walking past with a basket of rice on her head is frightened by the singing and wild appearance. Her rice falls slowly onto the ground. She screams and runs away—as if she had seen a demon.

I wake up. I am surrounded by a pack of children.

"Darimana, darimana?" they ask.

"Dari Sindu," I answer, as everyone laughs.

I am anxious to get back to the village to recuperate. I walk another few hours. I'm not far from the village now. An old man urgently stops me. The only words I can pick out are '*kawan sakit.*' Did he just tell me that my friend is sick?

Limping, I wade through the two streams and then up the hill. I can hear frantic rapping on the *kulkul* in the center of the village. What's happening?

More than 100 villagers crowd into Sadia's compound. Is a performance going on? From the terrified and confused looks on their faces, I can see that something's seriously wrong. I push through the crowd.

Eddie is totally naked with mud all over his body. His hands and feet are bound. He hops around, screaming and spitting at anyone who comes into range. I can't believe it. Is this a bad dream? Am I still asleep?

Eddie spins around three times, as if trying to build up energy, and then he charges the crowd. I barely recognize him.

Sadia appears from across the circle of onlookers. His arms are crossed, as if he's trying to holding himself together. He's frightened.

"I am sorry," Sadia murmurs. "I am sorry. Eddie is *gila* (insane)."

Smiling, he tries not to cry. He speaks in English and Balinese. I only catch fragments. He asks for help.

Crippled by my own exhaustion and mental confusion, I don't know what to do. Eddie screams at someone and tries to chase him. Everyone is looking at me, hoping I'll do something.

"Why is he tied up?" I ask Sadia. I can't bear to see Eddie tied. "Please untie him."

Sadia is clearly afraid. Eddie is like a wild animal. He jumps on the pavilion and roars at the crowd who shrink back. Eddie recoils and falls on the ground in a fetal position.

I walk over to Eddie. He looks at me lovingly, as if I am someone else. I don't think he knows who I am.

I walk back to the pavilion and sit down with my head in my hands. An inner voice comes to me.

Eddie mirrors the minds of his captors. If they are frightened, then he becomes Fear. It he is treated roughly, he becomes Rough. Cause and effect. When he is believed to be very dangerous, he is Danger personified. Be careful what you think, for that is what you will manifest in him.

"He's gone amok," groans Sadia.

Eddie is not the first Westerner to have run amok. There are many stories about people going mad in Bali. After hearing what Eddie has done, I am surprised the villagers didn't kill him. But then the people of Sindu love him.

Later, Eddie is tied down and confined to his bed. From time to time, I hear a scream or a murmur. The crowd is gone. Sadia and some of the painters remain on guard. I piece together what has happened from Sadia.

I leave for Gunung Agung. An hour later, Eddie gives all his possessions to Ota.

He takes the young painters with him to Denpasar. Most had never been to town before. At the market Eddie purchases baskets and clay pots. He fills them with wire, metal rods, and other hardware. He says he's being psychically guided to do the right thing. He buys cowboy hats—one for each member of his posse.

The painters want to go home, but there is one final stop. The Temple of the West. Armed with the last of his funds, he storms the hotel lobby. Money is his magical weapon.

Eddie leads the posse into the Bali Hai Hotel, grabs the first tourist he sees, says, "Welcome to Bali," and tries to stuff hundred dollar bills into his mouth.

The rebellion is quickly put down by the hotel manager and security guards. Eddie is bodily thrown out the door, but not before he lobs more hundred dollar bills like grenades at his challengers. Tourists run for cover.

Did he want to kidnap hotel guests? Take over the enemy's headquarters? I hope the police don't start looking for him.

Eddie returns to the village with the painters and his bizarre purchases. All of his money is gone. All he has left is a sarong, t-shirt and sandals. Now he has discarded even these.

He made more rice people and sat with them in the new house. He said he was afraid of the leyaks whom he believed were hunting him. He hid in the house and took off his clothes so that they might not see him.

When he thought the leyaks were near, like the Balinese, Eddie bent forward and looked back through his legs—naked. By reacting to the villagers as if they were leyaks and exposing himself, he's crossed the line into what is taboo.

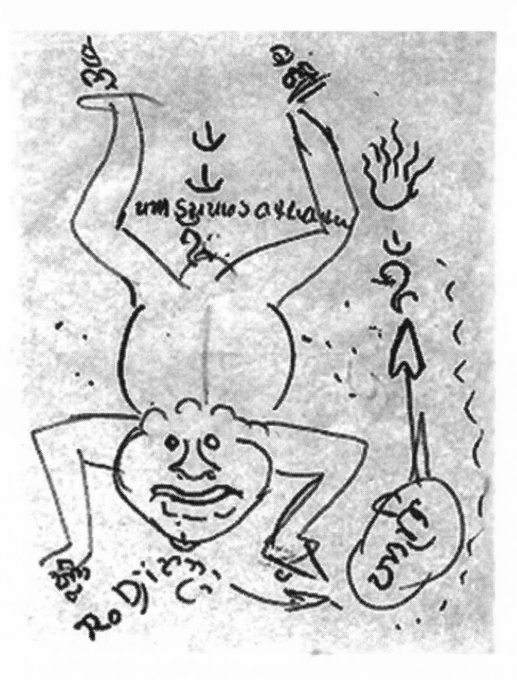

I look in on Eddie. He recognizes me and seems to have calmed down. I ask Sadia if we can untie him. Reluctantly he agrees. I try talking to Eddie, but he is in his own world.

"Eddie, are you all right?" He says nothing.

"What happenned at the hotel?"

"Tourists are the children of Rangda," he says, winding up.

"That's okay, Eddie. Never mind. As long as you are feeling better..."

"They must destroy everything. Without death there can be no new life," he say, leaping to his feet, as if somebody else has inhabited his body. He bolts for the door, runs out of the hut, and sprints deep into the village. Several painter-guards take up the chase. But he's disappeared. Dozens of people run through the village trying to find him. The kulkul sounds again. More people come and search. He's nowhere to be found. I return to the compound and see a light in the sky.

"Oh, my god. The house!"

We run to the new house, which is now aflame. The thatched roof is quickly consumed. Eddie is dancing around it. He sees us, runs, and tries to leap over a compound wall when six men corner him. Eddie screams and twists and turns. Suddenly, one of the painters, Madra, goes into trance and begins thrashing about the ground. The other painters are confused, frightened.

They charge and wrestle Eddie to the ground. A priest revives the trance victim with holy water. Then they all bring Eddie to Sadia's compound. The priest sprinkles the holy water on Eddie trying to bring him out of trance but it doesn't work. He is still delirious.

Sadia says this has been going on since yesterday, when he tried to set fire to the temple doors. He exposed himself, which momentarily kept everyone back, as they believed he might be a leyak. Whenever they'd approach, he'd flash them.

"We must keep him tied," says Sadia sadly.

Eddie tosses and turns and speaks an incoherent mixture of Balinese, Indonesian, French, German, Russian, Hebrew, and English. Boisterously he sings songs he learned in the seminary.

"God's love will shine tonight."

He makes word associations from whatever people say.

"Sarong, so wrong, so what, sow what, sarong?

Neighboring villagers have heard about the incident and begin coming to see what's happenned. Big Swede is among them.

He takes all this in with his usual aloofness, then offers 'pearls of wisdom' to comfort me.

"The journey of the mystic and the psychotic transcend ordinary reality and are often indistinguishable from each other," says the Enlightened One.

"So?" I ask, "what should we do?"

"You don't have to do anything. Learn from your friend's courage to confront the unknown."

"Sorry, Swede, I don't have time for metaphysics right now. I only want to help Eddie."

Eddie is smart. Real smart. He learned Balinese language and customs quickly. He also knows what is taboo and what isn't. Yet something in him makes him want to test the limits. I'm not sure that Eddie has taken the path of the mystic. I think he's flipped out. But who am I to judge?

A few hours have passed. Eddie has moments of lucidity. For half an hour, he acts as if nothing had happened. Has the nightmare passed? We talk.

"Eddie, you scared me. I was afraid you'd hurt yourself or someone else. How are you feeling?"

Eddie tries to sit up but the ropes keep him down. I roll up a sarong for a pillow and put it under his head.

"Don't be angry with me. You had to climb the mountain. I had to climb my mountain. Ota will show me the way."

Eddie's given up everything—possessions, customs, money, and now his own sanity. For what?

"I journey with the ancestors now and do what they tell me."

The forces from within him are rising again, powerful and dangerous.

"Eddie, please don't go into trance again. Sooner or later someone will get hurt."

"I can't help myself. It's not mine to stop," he wails.

I'm to blame. I've seen this build up in Eddie since he arrived in Bali. For months, he's been trying to find a sacred experience that would remake him. I encouraged him. I didn't believe he'd actually be able to go into trance, but now he's found the way. It's taken him over.

He wanted a transformative experience. Well, he got what we wished for.

Eddie rolls his eyes back and tightens his jaw. Pressure is building up again and he's about to give birth to it.

"Where's Ota? I want to see Ota!" he cries.

"He's not here now. No one has seen him," I explain.

Eddie sits up straight, rolls his eyes up, then closes them as if going into trance again.

What did Ota tell him? Ota now has Eddie's money and possessions. In exchange, Eddie is on his own without a guide. Ota probably has no idea how much Eddie needs help right now. I beg Sadia to locate Ota.

"Maybe he can tell us what's going on."

Sadia looks as if he'd just eaten something bitter.

There is something compelling about Eddie's total willingness to follow his passion wherever it takes him.

Big Swede says, "You're the crazy one. You're trying to make Eddie conform to your limited reality, your rules. He's the courageous one risking it all."

I can't chase Eddie when he escapes again. I'm still too sore and bruised from my climb. He screams from afar when they catch him. He sounds like a condemned animal. When he's re-tied, I sleep until there's another outburst. The next capture is accompanied by a howl.

Eddie goes deeper. And gains more strength every time he spins around. It's unbearable. *Drama Maka* has been replaced with *Drama Gila.* Balinese come from nearby villages to see the freak.

In all the temples throughout the village, women are making offerings and praying. Priests put offerings all around the compound, in the hut, under Eddie's bed, and sprinkle us frequently with holy water. The village is obsessed with quelling the gods. Everywhere people are sick with terrible headaches and vomiting.

"Nick, I've had a hard-on for days," Eddie says. "This energy in me, you cannot imagine. I can see and hear everything. I can move the clouds. Look! My body *is* the web of life."

Weeks ago we were in paradise, and now we're plunged into some kind of Hell. I am finally in Bali and my oldest friend is flipping out; spitting at priests, squatting bare-assed in mud puddles, burning huts, and cursing in seven languages. Will the village turn on us? What about the Devauxes? Will they find out who kidnapped them? What about the Bali Hai Hotel incident? The Kuta villagers? The police?

Night finally comes. Eddie moans in the next room. Exhausted from my pilgrimage, I keep waking up. I go out onto the porch. This was our refuge from danger. Now the danger is here.

The porch is filled with dozens of unfinished paintings. It's overwhelming. Demons, horrible monsters. Fangs, claws, blood. Bulbous eyes watch me as I stand naked in the night. The paintings are everywhere—on the walls, on the floor, in the rafters, in our rooms, stacked up against the wall.

Sadia walks out of the shadows. He can't sleep either. He says what's happened to Eddie is a horrendous omen. The gods are angry. Maybe the volcano will erupt.

"Did I make an offering and say the prayer?" he asks. I lie and say "yes." He looks relieved. I was entrusted with a simple task and didn't do it.

Chapter 26

ROPE TRICKS

Eddie's magical powers multiply. "I've learned the ropes! Watch! I hold the sarong in my teeth," he says. "And pass it over the ropes and the knots come undone. Voilà!"

It's unbelievable! Eddie really can untie any knot the Balinese can tie. Eddie moans, cries, and laughs, and after a few minutes or an hour, he will eventually untie any knot!

He moves his hands into mudra positions and then says to the painters in Indonesian, "Tie it as tight as you can. Make it hurt. My thought processes are more powerful. You tie them; I untie them with my mind."

This game goes on for maybe two or three days. I lose track of time. Whenever anyone comes into his room, Eddie, still tied, kicks or spits rice. Sometimes he whispers to himself like a child that's been sent to his room. Other times he sings, "Manic depression, blow straight and miss" in the style of Jimi Hendrix, or "Take another little piece of my heart, now baby," like Janice Joplin. Sometimes he sounds just like them.

I drift in and out of nightmares, as Eddie's voices enter my dreams. I get no rest. Eddie hasn't slept in days. He's skin and bones. The painters take turns on watch. Some stand guard on the porch. The village routine has stopped.

A week passes. More people come to see the "crazy Westerner," as word spreads to villages even further away.

One morning, two policemen come into the village. I watch through the compound gate, making sure they don't see me. Eddie is still tied up on the bed. Quiet for the moment. They walk through the village and then back again. I guess everyone was able to divert their attention. Sadia comes in.

"Do they know about Eddie?" I ask.

"Yahh, but they don't want him. They are looking for some Balinese guys who kidnapped your friends. Don't worry. They will find them. Bali is very small."

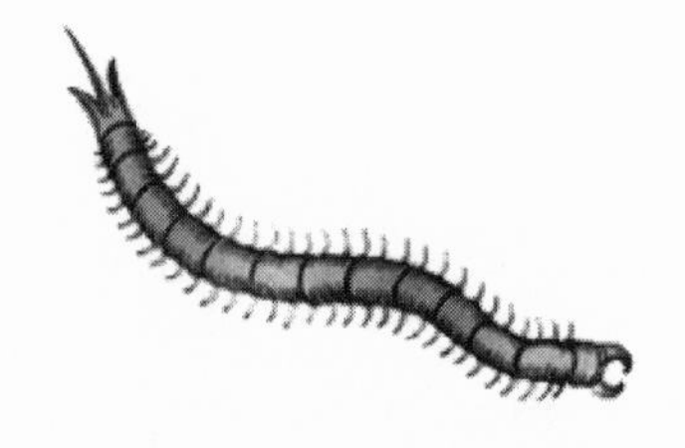

Eddie is burning up with fever. Sadia applies *obat*—a kind of gooey white paste—to Eddie's forehead. A pedanda (priest) then chants a mantra onto a leaf and sticks the leaf in the obat. They do everything they can to alleviate his fever and his madness. Eddie spits in the priest's face.

Sadia's wife, the painters' wives, and the other women make offerings in the temple despite their dreadful chronic headaches. Exhausted, they've been on vigil praying since the first outburst. They must pacify the gods for the transgressions they made, which they believe caused this misfortune.

Madness has amplified Eddie's brilliance. He plays mind games with me, Sadia, and the priests who come to heal him. What makes it hard is that he easily outsmarts us and he seems to read our minds. He's always ahead of us. I try to talk him back to his senses. He tells me to "buzz off." I threaten to leave him to fend for himself.

"Won't you save me, beautiful sir?" he says, smiling sweetly.

Priests come again with a tub filled with holy water from the mother temple at Besakih. Eddie is tied to the bamboo cross and lowered into the water. It's his cue to play the resurrection scene as his apostles bathe him.

He whispers, his voice hoarse from yelling, "And Rangda came unto me and said, 'Go then, seek something that is impossible to find, something about which nothing is known. Approach the darkness. Find out what it wants.'"

It is an incredible drama. *Drama Mandi.*

He twists in agony on the cross and cries in pain.

When the priests lift him into a bath, he spits. The priests calmly wipe the spittle from their faces and pour more holy water over his head. They care lovingly for him.

Maybe this is some kind of Balinese black magic. Maybe another village is jealous of our stay in Sindu. Maybe they found out about Eddie stealing the mask and someone put a curse on him. Maybe Ota. If it is, then certainly a white magic shaman can get rid of it.

I ask Sadia to call Wayan Linah, the most powerful *dukun* in Bali, to drive away the black magic. An hour later, Big Swede and Wayan Linah arrive. I'm glad, very glad to see him. He greets me warmly and enters the hut. He looks at Eddie, who is strapped to the bed cursing incoherently.

I expect an elaborate exorcism ritual to chase away Eddie's demons. Linah waves a branch of orange blossoms back and forth over Eddie's body. Its fragrance fills the room. Linah bends down and blows in Eddie's left ear, whispering slowly, asking the spirit to identify itself, its purpose, and to come out. He shakes the branch over all of Eddie's orifices while chanting in Balinese:

Searching and praying with the sweet smell,
waving the flowers and probing.
The leaves are shaking.
My hand and mind while divining the sickness
Is searching and praying.
Searching and probing
for the body that roams with the spirits.
Roams with the spirits.
Follows the demons.
I call for you to come to the flowers
to better smell its breath.
Tell us of our insufficiencies and
we shall increase our offerings.
Come and talk.
Come smell the sweet blossom.

No answer. Linah stands and turns to leave.

"Wait," I cry out. "Is that it?"

With absolute certainty, Linah says, "No spirit come, no demons. Tidak tau."

"It can't be," I plead. "I need it to be Balinese magic so that you can heal him. Please...try the other ear."

Linah comes back in, kneels over Eddie, and blows in the other ear, again whispering evocations to the alleged demon or possessor. No answer.

Linah stands, looks at me and says, "Not Balinese black magic. Maybe from America. You understand."

Eddie closes his eyes. No other hopes, no other alternatives. Except retreat.

Just then, one of the young boys brings in Rangda's necklace and hands it to Linah.

"He found this near your house? Where's the mask?" asks Linah.

"Eddie took it from a temple in Kuta. I don't know where he keeps it."

He says something to the boy, who runs out calling some of the men to a search.

"Must have Barong energy to balance," continues Linah. "Must find Rangda mask and make ceremony."

On that, Eddie sits up.

"Eddie, where did you hide the Rangda mask?" I ask, "Please tell us."

On that, he flips out and begins screaming and twisting, trying to break free and reach for the necklace.

Linah throws a magical black-and-white cloth over the necklace and hurries out of the compound.

It is morning. It's just getting light and it's quiet. Eddie kicks his feet against the bamboo wall softly but repeatedly, as if sending an SOS. He calls out to Ota by chanting.

This morning there is no "Nipas" coffee ritual. A painter sleeps on the porch. No one has painted for nearly two weeks. I'm hungry. I walk across the compound to the kitchen house and find a banana. I don't recognize my own shadow against the wall. I've lost a lot of weight. I look like a puppet.

Eddie has stopped banging. I look in. His hands are bloodied from the rope. He looks at me and very quietly asks me to untie him. He doesn't look crazy. The intensity is gone from his face. His eyes are no longer dilated. Another period of lucidity.

A few hours pass. He's still quiet and asks me to untie him. I ask Sadia. Maybe he's better. We both look at Eddie.

"I want something to eat," he says.

A good sign. I untie Eddie and take him outside. He pulls his sarong around him and we sit on the porch of the hut next to ours.

I bring him a banana and feed him a piece at a time. Sadia goes to get some rice. Sadia's wife makes coffee and brings it out on a tray. Eddie looks tired. We talk softly.

"You okay?" I ask, more than a little afraid he's not and might try something violent.

"Yeah, I'm okay," he says.

"I'm glad, Eddie, I'm glad."

It's the first time that there has been a pause. Maybe it's over.

"Eddie, I've worried that you'd hurt yourself...or someone. I'm sorry you were tied up," I explain.

"I've seen the Truth, Nick. The truth," declares Eddie, his passion building. "Death isn't to be feared. It's the soil from which new life will grow."

"I'm sorry, Eddie. I just don't see..."

"Listen," he interrupts whispering, "I was wrong to stop tourists. Instead, I must help them destroy Bali. Then transformation will come."

"I know you don't believe that Bali must be destroyed."

"Yes, it must. Trying to save Bali is the real madness," says Eddie, as his fingers fidget and twitch.

"Sure, Eddie."

Better placate him. I can't risk getting him angry.

"Maybe our time here is up. Maybe we should go home. See your mom and dad.." I probe gently.

"This *is* my home. I have work to do here."

"Yes, but, maybe we need to rest and get back to familiar things," I rationalize. "I've thought it over and..."

He leaps on me. "You bastard!" he yells, "you goddamn traitor!"

He pulls my hair hard and wrestles me to the ground. I try to push him back, but he's like a steel spring. He holds down my shoulders with both arms, plunges his head into my leg, and bites.

The pain is awful. He doesn't let go. I twist and smash his head again and again with my elbow. His teeth are still clenched like a pit bull. Someone gives Eddie a big kick. Eddie lets me go and charges them. Another chase.

I lie there for a few moments until the pain subsides. I sit up. Oh, it hurts. Afraid to look, I pull back the sarong. My leg is bleeding badly. A hunk of flesh hangs from my thigh. I press it back. Sadia's wife brings something to wrap around my leg. I try to stand. I'm shaking. I fall.

Five minutes later, Eddie is brought back.

"You'll never catch me, the real me. Never," he taunts.

"You asshole, you're just an asshole," I swear. "I've had enough of your crap. You can rot in hell for all I care."

I rush to the hut. My leg is killing me. Goddamn it! Let him kill himself. Let him set the village on fire. It's not my problem.

I grab my shoulder bag but it catches on the hook. I pull it. Still caught. I give it a yank and half the bamboo wall pulls out. Goddamn it. I grab my camera, and journal, and the few things I have left. Everything goes into the bag, and I'm out the door.

Sadia follows me. "Sadia, I can't take this anymore. He wants to stay in Bali. Fine, he can stay. I'm leaving."

Sadia is stunned.

"I'm sorry, I can't help." I reach out to shake Sadia's hand but he just stands there. Never mind. I turn and limp out of the village as fast as I can. Perfect timing. There's a bemo on the road. I hop on. It's headed to North Bali. Fine, anywhere. Just get me outta here.

The bemo bounces further north, picking up and dropping off people as it goes. The air becomes cooler as we gain altitude, heading toward Batur volcano. "It's definitely *kaja.* We are headed toward the gods." I begin to relax and remember.

Eddie and I sit on the small veranda of our cheap hotel in Hong Kong, recalling our high school band days and friends we knew. Those days are over and we each have new lives ahead of us..

"My father is no longer calling the shots," Eddie says.

My old friend and I are both starting over. A fresh slate. A clean start.

The warm sun is low in the sky, casting strong shadows. Hundreds of people line the roadside. Everyone is dressed in their finest. The bemo moves slowly. A procession is headed our way. The bemo divides the procession. Men to one side of the road, women on the other. I look at the approaching women. In the front are the youngest girls, then teenagers, and the older women in the rear. As we pass, every girl or woman looks at me for just a split second. Each face registers in my consciousness. In the faces of hundreds of women I see the entire life cycle of the Balinese woman metamorphosized and aged: from six and seven years old, through puberty, adolescence, adulthood, and old age.

As each woman looks into my eyes—for that moment—I see her essence and the soul of all Balinese women. It is profoundly, unbearably beautiful, the quintessential Balinese woman. She looks like the girl in the mirror!!

Dear Nicholas,

... Do you know what the "anima" is? It's your woman within and without.

Jung says a man's anima is the female personification of all the feminine psychological tendencies in a man's psyche. All your vague feelings, moods, prophetic hunches, receptiveness to the irrational, capacity to love, feeling for nature, and your relation to the unconscious—that's your feminine side.

Honor it and your anima's manifestations—the women you meet—because the anima contains the possibility of achieving wholeness.

Love, Sonny

About a kilometer past the procession, there is a turn. Off the side of the road are several jeeps with soldiers. They are questioning two young guys on a motorcycle. Soldiers! I've got to get back.

I wait until we are around the next bend, and then have the bemo driver stop and let me off. I catch another bemo south to Klungkung. It will take several hours before I get back to the village. I hope I'm in time. If the soldiers, or police, or immigration get to Eddie before I do, no telling what they'll do to him.

As I get near Sindhu, I stop. There's Sadia, Wayan Linah, and Big Swede. The painters are trying to load Eddie into a bemo. Sadia tells me that soldiers are looking for Eddie. They must move him. But where?

I've got it. Perhaps Dr. Li in Klungkung can help Eddie! He works with mental patients. He must know what to do. Sadia is quick to agree and promises me that the women and priests will pray for Eddie, wherever he is.

The ropes that tie Eddie to the bamboo pole fall off. He's done it again. The painters grab him and try to hold him down. He twists and cries in pain. Suddenly, his eyes roll back in his head. My god, they've hurt him. I run up beside him. He collapses. His breathing subsides and his whole body relaxes. As I prop up his head, I feel how incredibly hot it is, almost too hot to touch. I set him down.

Linah whispers, "Special trance. Maybe God Siwa. You understand?"

Eddie opens his eyes. He is peaceful. He says, "Love. It's love. I am no longer a prisoner. I am free."

We'll see about that. The soldiers could be back any minute. The painters load Eddie in the back of the bemo.

Chapter 27

KLUNGKUNG

Thirty minutes later, the bemo stops in Klungkung—a former prisoner-of-war camp during the Japanese occupation. Dr. Li comes out of the makeshift mental hospital. We're back. Everything is coming full circle. Like a bad dream, we are retracing our steps to find our way home.

Dr. Li walks with a limp. His bright, clean face is contrasted by a soiled gray smock. His hospital has no resources and a miniscule staff. It is evident that he is overworked.

I tell Dr. Li about Eddie, but he's already heard. Eddie is quiet, distracted by these new surroundings. In a small, all-white building, there is one rectangular barracks with six beds; an adjoining room has another six beds. A woman appears and puts her arms through the bars.

"Sir, sir, beautiful sir, can you see me? Can you save me?

I look away. No other patients are here. Dr. Li explains that they are all in the Crafts Center during the day. Eddie sits on the side of a bed. His hands are still tied. Is his magic wearing off or is Eddie just not trying to untie the knots?

Dr. Li tries to examine him and asks questions.

"Has he eaten any mushrooms?"

"None, this has nothing to do with psychedelics," I reply.

"What about water? You drink water in the village?"

"No, not much, we are afraid of dysentery. We only drink a little tea and coffee," I explain.

"He's very skinny and probably dehydrated."

He checks Eddie's pulse and looks at his eyes and tongue. Eddie begins to examine Dr. Li back, in a game of "doctor."

"What do you eat in the village?" Dr. Li asks Eddie.

It is an exercise in futility. Eddie seems to be absolutely normal, but on the inside he is nervous, jittery—as if his world is moving three times faster than ours. Eddie eventually twists the interview around so that he is questioning Dr. Li. Eddie is far too clever. A few weeks ago he had read *Symbols of Transformation.* Now he is playing Jung to Dr. Li's Freud.

Dr. Li gives Eddie some tranquilizer pills to help him sleep. Eddie gets excited again. Eddie pretends to take them. When Li turns his back, Eddie winks at me and spits the pills out the open window. It's our little secret, and I am a coconspirator. Li takes me back to his office near the road.

Dr. Li assures me that he'll be able to help Eddie.

"We have a very high success rate with cases like this."

I'm not so sure.

"What is it? Why did this happen?"

Dr. Li leans back in his chair and puts the tips of his fingers together.

"Could be many things. Stress mostly, I imagine. What do you think? Has he a strong ego? A weak ego?"

"Oh, very strong. He's always out there, talking with people incessantly, making quick commitments, doing things."

"Ahh...weak ego," he nods knowingly.

"A weak ego?"

"Yes, a weak ego is always trying to find itself. It needs a lot of acknowledgement. He identifies with others? He's impressionable, right? Gets involved with people around him? His mind flits from one thing to the next? Never finishes anything?"

"Yes."

"Ah...Bali is very stressful for weak egos. People always asking you where you are going, where you are from. Western people aren't used to these personal questions constantly. It's overwhelming...then there's the dehydration. Dysentery. Yes, many stressors."

"The best thing to do is to take him home?"

"Yes, but in the meantime, let's see if we can find some drugs."

There's nothing more I can do. Dr. Li suggests I return to the village and come back tomorrow.

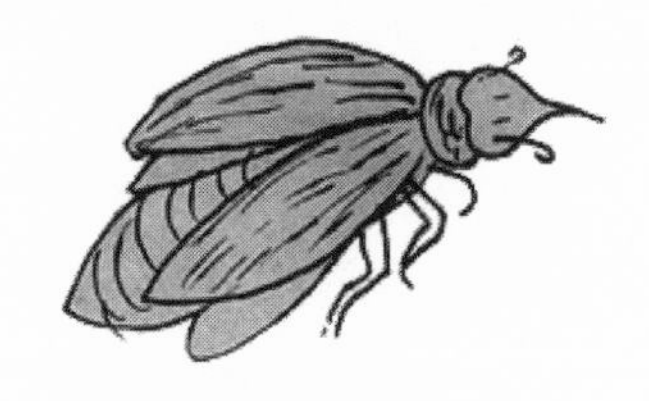

I spend the night in the village. I can't sleep. Sadia's up as well. It's ironic that after all this, we never spent one night in the new house.

Sadia and I walk out to the house. Under the charred rubble I find the hole that Eddie's dug in its center (he called it "the navel of the house"), where he buried a pot, some wire, some of his scrolls, and our damaged camera. Sadia says that when I was on the volcano, Eddie climbed into the rafters and sighted the full moon through a bamboo-pole telescope. I take Eddie's ritual objects from the house and return them to the hut. Sadia puts some *obat* on my leg.

How can I get Eddie back to the States? I have less than $100; Eddie has nothing.

I have no other options. In the morning, I go to Sanur to find Pierre Devaux. He lent us his camera; maybe he'll lend me money for airplane tickets. I find him at the scene of the crime in the Bali Hai Hotel. When I tell him what has happened, he is sympathetic. I promise to repay him when I get back to the States. Just as he is about to lend me the money, his wife, Nicole, comes down from their room. She sits in the chair beside me. Staring at me. She looks at my ring, then into my eyes. She knows! Pierre says something in French, and they begin to argue. Then Nicole gets up and leaves. Pierre looks at me and says he's sorry. So am I.

I close my eyes and "see" a kind of daydream.

Eddie is being tied to his bed. Dr. Li discovers a huge pile of pills outside the window and changes his strategy. Now they shoot Eddie up with tranquilizers. I see a guy from the bed opposite Eddie climb in and out of the window, hiding things and then gleefully finding them again.

I go to the airline ticket office in the hotel and make reservations without money. The clerk checks Eddie's name and asks where we are staying.

"In Sindu village." How stupid of me.

From the hotel, I try to contact Eddie's father. He's not in Indiana. He's in Europe. His office gives me a telex number. I pare down our situation to its essential facts. EDDIE IS SICK. WE NEED TO RETURN TO THE STATES. PLEASE PREPAY 2 TICKETS FROM BALI TO SAN FRANCISCO. THANK YOU.

I'm so tired that I can't stop the daydreams.

In the beds next to Eddie are Sancho Panza and Don Quixote look-alikes: a fat Chinese servant, and his skinny master. The Chinese guy's wife comes in. She's a shrew. Being crazy was obviously his only escape.

I return to the village. Eddie is the main topic of conversation. The buzz is greater than ever. The police know about the missing mask, the incident at the hotel, the burning of the hut. They want to put him in jail! I have to get him *out of Bali.* Now!

When I return to the hospital in Klungkung, Dr. Li takes me to the Crafts Center in a nearby building to see Eddie. He seems at ease. He's supervising the other patients. He goes from one person to the next and comments on their various art projects. I sit by the door and watch. He seems a bit better.

Eddie and I go for a walk around the grounds. Like a weather vane twisting in the wind, Eddie goes in and out of trance with almost no warning.

For a few minutes he has a moment of lucidity.

"Listen, you have to get me out of here," he pleads. "That guy, the assistant, the one who gives me shot? He tweaks my penis every chance he gets, like they do to the little kids here."

Is this true? I can't tell anymore.

Then he starts talking again about love and the generator. Not this again. He speaks slowly and clearly.

"Everything in nature operates on the principle of vibrations. The generator is only a physical manifestation of what we ourselves are capable of when we generate love. With love you can lift the stones from the temple. You can travel to distant places. You can heal. Where there is love, there is energy, creative energy. This is the secret I've been given."

I believe him. Now I'm going nuts too.

"Did you know that when there is fear, there is no room for love? I've been devoured by Rangda and died. Now there is only love."

His gaze shifts inward. He sees things that I can't. As we walk under a towering tree, he points up at the sun and looks directly at it.

"I can suck up the love energy of the sun through my eyes." He turns to me. "So can you!"

We walk into the communal bedroom. The fat Chinese servant collects the one and only bedpan from a thin Indian. Eddie nods to him and then says to me, "That's Krishnamurti." Only his white hair and thinness make him look anything like the Indian master. This is Eddie's new guru. They signal each other with their eyebrows. Krishnamurti looks at the clouds through the window, then back at Eddie.

"Krishnamurti shows me the details in God's work." Eddie sniffs the air, like an animal before a storm. He looks up at the clouds.

"There, the sun, the clouds...ahhhhhh," Eddie sighs. Krishnamurti and Eddie are in another world, sharing private moments. Suddenly, the whole room gets brighter and brighter and brighter. I rub my eyes. Then it's normal again. Krishnamurti winks at me.

We're wasting precious time. The police could arrive any minute. I have to talk to Eddie again about returning to the States. Before I say anything, he reads my mind.

"How can you even think it?" he asks me. "There is no other place like this in the world. Even *you* know Bali is the doorway in. All things are possible here. Don't even try."

Eddie complains about his left leg where Dr. Li has given him tranquilizer injections. The shots have made the leg puff up. It is so sore that Eddie limps around.

"I'm just like Dr. Li," says Eddie. "He's deliberately made me just like him. Look, we both limp on the same foot."

Eddie leans over and whispers to me. He says, "They do awful things to me at night, bad things." Eddie sings and moves his hands, twisting them above his head.

"The itsy-bitsy spider went up the water spout!" He contorts his face and body. "Down came the rain and washed the spider out." He throws his arms down as God would throw rain down upon the earth. "Out came the sun..." He stares into the sunlight and stops. Then he turns and whispers, "...and dried up all the rain." And then building..."And the itsy-bitsy spider went up the spout again." He is stretching his body up higher and higher.

"The truth is everywhere, Nick. Everywhere I look, I see that the creative power of the universe is love."

It's exhausting to be with him. He desperately wants me, wants all of us, to see his reality.

Eddie's only been here two days, but it seems like forever. He wants to go back to the village. Dr. Li tells me that the drugs are helping him sleep. They don't have to tie him down anymore. The exhausted Dr. Li tries to instill confidence.

Eddie's leg is much worse. He can barely walk.

"I can't let the shots get to my mind so I hold it in my leg," he explains. "That's why it's so bad. Just tell them to stop. I will hold it here until my leg falls off. I have to protect my brain."

Eddie is enraged so he is tied to the bed. His wrists are chafed and bleeding. I can't stand seeing him deteriorate.

Eddie is not getting better; he looks terrible and has lost a lot of weight. Dr. Li takes me to his office near the road. He proudly unveils a strange device. I recognize it from high school physics class. It's a spark generator. It has a crank with two big wheels that rub together and two rods with some wires coming off of them. Dr. Li dusts off an old manual.

It is in English, written in 1947, on shock therapy! He's going to try it on Eddie.

"*Tidak bisa*," I tell him. (No way.) I assure him that Eddie and I will be on our way back to the States very soon.

In the last light of an unusually hot afternoon, two young Balinese soldiers come in. Their uniforms are immaculate, not a wrinkle or a spot. They want to take Eddie to their office for questioning. They aren't saying what it's about. Dr. Li admonishingly tells them that Eddie is very sick—perhaps even contagious. Do they want to infect the officers? Their inexperience slows them down.

The look at Eddie's file which contains only his passport and a registration form. They write the passport number down and then leave. Dr. Li says they'll be back in the morning with their superiors.

Before leaving, I go to check on Eddie one last time. No one is in the ward. Where are they? I check the Crafts Center. All the windows are covered with cardboard.

I open the door and enter the darkened room. Eddie is in the center of the room with a group of patients. He's showing them a magic trick? But when I get closer, I see he's built a miniature "generator"! There is a stack of junk and tangle of wires. Two rods stick in the air.

Eddie chants at low vibration. Then he stands up. In each hand is a glass tumbler with tinfoil wrapped over the top of it. He moves about strangely. A jerky *Topeng* dance. Is he going into trance? He moves around the circle of patients. And then...and then! A faint, fog-like glow begins to come from each of the tumblers. The patients cheer. He dances, moving faster and faster. The tumbler illuminates their faces with an eerie green glow. He holds the tumblers up and looks at me.

Chapter 28

ESCAPE

Back in the village, I turn up the oil lamp and gather what little is left of our possessions and stuff them into a basket. A camera, a cassette recorder, my journal, some clothes. Scraps of Eddie's writings are pasted onto maps and rolled up into scrolls. They are scattered everywhere. The place is a mess. I gather anything up that might help a psychiatrist one day.

Sadia finishes rolling up a hundred paintings and gives them to me. "You sell these in America and come back," he says proudly.

"Okay, Sadia. Okay, I will."

Several boys pack all the stuff in the back of the chartered bemo and prepare to pick up Eddie, then head for the airport. Sadia knows I don't want to leave. I am bound to this place forever. There is a catch in the back of my throat. It's a sad moment. Our time together is over. I can't look anyone in the eye. Awkwardly, Lobo, Rani, Madra, Gitah, Kokoh, and Linah, all gather around. No one says anything. The village itself is psychically drained. The curse from the gods requires more offerings, more prayers, more time.

Just then, some boys bring Dr. Li into the compound.

"What happened? Is something wrong? Where's Eddie?" I shout.

"He's escaped. I thought he might come back here?"

My mind races.

"Where could he be? Where would he go?"

I run toward our burnt-down house. The full moon illuminates the charred ruins. There is Eddie sitting cross-legged. The Rangda mask at his side. I walk closer. He is fooling with the rolling machine.

"Want one?" he inquires.

"No thanks, I don't smoke."

"Me neither, I just like making them."

It's dawn. We are on the porch for the last time. I go to the well to clean up. I pick up the mirror. She's not there.

Sadia, Linah, and the painters gather around. Eddie sits on the mats; he hasn't said anything. He looks sad and worn. Finally he speaks.

"*Ma'af kan sekali. Ma'afkan sekali,*" he says.

Sadia says, "There is nothing to forgive. Good and bad are in everybody. It's a gift from God so that we may learn to perfect ourselves."

Sadia's son hurries in. He says soldiers are coming from the South. The chartered bemo is on the North road. We still have time to escape.

We run through the village path to the bemo. Sadia says they'll follow in a truck.

The morning light encourages the tufts of new rice.

Watching the roadside slip away, Eddie becomes anxious again.

"I don't want to leave. Please. Not yet."

"Eddie, the soldiers and police are looking for you."

"But you can't go back. The draft."

"It's okay. Can't run away forever."

The bemo arrives at the airport. I go to the counter. The clerk can't find the prepaid tickets. He goes in the back room.

"Come on, come on."

"Our house," he says, "our house was stillborn."

Sadia, Kokoh, Lobo, Rani, Madra, Suweca, Madé Gitah, and Linah stand awkwardly around the lobby. It's the first time anyone, except for Sadia, has been to an airport.

Outside in the parking lot, I spy Ota. He sheepishly looks away. A truck pulls up and a dozen Balinese soldiers get out.

The clerk comes back with the tickets.

"Yes, come on. Hurry, hurry."

The clerk puts baggage tags on my baskets and the roll of paintings. I return to the group with my bag. Eddie is breathing heavily.

"I'm going to be saved. Two white horses will come. For me and my princess. I'll never leave Bali. Never," says Eddie.

Oh, not this again. Only a few more steps.

I present our boarding passes and passports to the gate attendant. The attendant examines Eddie in his dirty t-shirt, sarong, and sandals. He looks considerably different from the button-downed seminarian in his passport photo. The attendant checks the visa, stamps the passport.

We all walk out to the tarmac. Gamelan music strikes up. A few yards behind us, a small quartet of Balinese musicians play genders. A young woman throws flower petals from a small basket. "Welcome to Bali," she says.

The small plane turns on its engines. The painters recoil, frightened. I turn and hug each one. Then I embrace Sadia.

"Om shanti shanti, my dear friend," I say.

The seconds are slipping away. I can't believe this is it.

I can see the soldiers inside the terminal.

"No, I want to stay," says Eddie.

I take a chance. I hold open my shoulder bag. Eddie looks down and sees the rice people.

"It's over, Eddie. We're going home." The resistance passes as his eyes soften.

I put my arm around Eddie and move us toward the plane. He says, "I'm going to freak out."

"No, Eddie," I say softly, "You'll be okay now. Say good-bye."

Eddie looks back at the group of painters as they wave. There are no white horses, no Balinese princesses, only sad brown faces in cowboy hats.

Eddie puts his arm around me, and says weakly, "I couldn't help myself."

"I know, Eddie. I understand."

I help him up the stairs and into the plane.

Chapter 29

North Hollywood, California, 1995
EPILOGUE

Now the guests arrive. A dark-haired woman, illuminated by an oil lamp, fixes a frangipani behind each person's ear as they enter, and whispers, "Welcome to Bali."

I am standing in the backyard, lighting the torches. There's a full moon just barely visible through the lemon trees; the scent of their flowers permeates the air. I can feel the pulse of the earth under my feet. I know tonight is very special. A night like no other.

My wife, acutely aware of the poetry of life, is in our small house preparing for the guests: straightening out our tea room where we have breakfast. A small room cluttered with stacks of first edition English novels, poetry books, fashion magazines. A few years ago we went to Bali together, and then I asked her to marry me. "Oh yes, please," she said.

We thought we were too old to start a family. But we discovered—adventurers and loners that we are—that we both wanted a child. We got the idea when I produced five PBS television specials. One program was on adoption. And that's how we created our family. Bronwyn wears the tiniest dress; ready for her one-month birthday.

In Bali they'd have a Topeng dance to celebrate this birthday, and so that's what we're doing. One hundred friends will soon fill the backyard.

As synchronicity would have it, a Topeng dancer and small gamelan group are passing through Los Angeles. Last night they performed at UCLA, and tomorrow they go to Hawaii for another performance, and then on to Australia. When I learned that they'd be in Los Angeles, I asked if them if they'd perform for Bronwyn's birthday.

Right now the dancer is preparing his masks and costumes behind an improvised curtain that we built this afternoon. More guests pour into the garden through the side gate. A cloud passes over the moon. It's almost pitch dark. My father and brother are visiting from Indiana. There's Merta, a Balinese dancer I haven't seen for a few years. Christine, who studied Balinese music with me in Berkeley in the mid-seventies. Peter, who has just finished a documentary on the Dali Lama of Tibet. And my old pal, Adrian whose new movie for Paramount is the nation's top moneymaker. Yoshi, a Japanese performance artist. And Sonny, who just got back from East Africa. And many other friends and colleagues.

My wife brings baby Bronwyn into the backyard and is quickly surrounded by admiring friends.

I'm very nervous. Some of the most intelligent and fascinating people I know fill the backyard. People take seats at the umbrella-covered tables which surround an open circle. To one side of the circle, is the curtain which will hide the dancer when he changes masks and costumes between scenes. Children sit on the ground and monopolize the best seats closest to the performance area. The adults stand and sit behind them.

A hand reaches out from behind the curtain and places an offering of flowers, rice, and incense on the ground and then disappears. The small gamelan ensemble begins playing an overture. I stand halfway behind the curtain and watch as the dancer says his mantras evoking the ancestors, and enters a light trance. I love this man. I know what it's taken for him to become a Topeng dancer and to be here for me, for my wife, and my baby. He's here to make this night special. The purpose of the dance is to exorcise any demonic spirits that may have been present when the baby's spirit entered the world. The performance will ensure that the child will have a blessed life.

I am deeply grateful.

"Salamat datang. Time to do your magic."

He raises the mask to his face and joins the power of the mask. "Chang, chang, pak, pak, CHANG!,"strikes the gamelan.

Baby Bronwyn jumps to attention. She gazes beyond her group of admirers and watches as the curtain begins to shake.

Long fingers reach out from the curtain then disappear. What's behind the curtain? The audience leans forward.

The dancer's movements are exceptionally good. He's an entertainer, shaman, and priest all in one. When he performs in Bali, people come from the surrounding villages. I was there when he put on a mask for the very first time.

According to Balinese religion, good and bad exist in all things: two sides of the same coin. Evil cannot be destroyed, so it must be appeased and brought under control. Many of the Balinese dramas and ceremonies are for this purpose. The dancer becomes an intermediary between humans and the gods, good and bad, who are all manifestations of the one Supreme God, Sanghyang Widhi Wasa.

From behind the curtain protrude the long, stiff vibrating fingernails of Rangda! Suddenly she leaps through the curtains and the crowd gasps. Her drooping breasts fling to the right as she spins. Someone screams. She stretches and her tongue rolls in her mouth and her eyes bulge out; her grotesqueness accentuated by the illumination from the torches. The musicians pound their wooden mallets on the bronze keys. Randga spins and spins. The children in the front row dash for safety. Randga laughs, as she terrifies and frightens the spectators.

"Anak, anak, enak, enak." Whom shall I feast on tonight?!!

Now the music slows, just the gongs and the light tapping of the drum is heard as Rangda surveys the audience.

Her eyes find baby Bronwyn, who stares back at the monster—calm and composed, having only a month ago descended from the gods. The power of her radiant goodness stops the demoness in her tracks. Humbly, Rangda puts her hands together and bows reverently to the human goddess. My friends cheer. They love it.

Behind the curtain, the dancer takes off the Rangda mask. Eddie wipes his face with a towel, then gives me that famous, irresistable smile. He prepares another mask to continue the performance. One man playing many parts.

Imagine, two boys in Bali. So young. So long ago. We were looking for something magical to bring meaning to our lives, and we found it.

At dawn, Eddie and his group fly to Hawaii where they will perform for the East-West Center. And baby Bronwyn will do what she's done every morning of her life: she will greet the day with a big smile, ready for whatever her world has to offer.

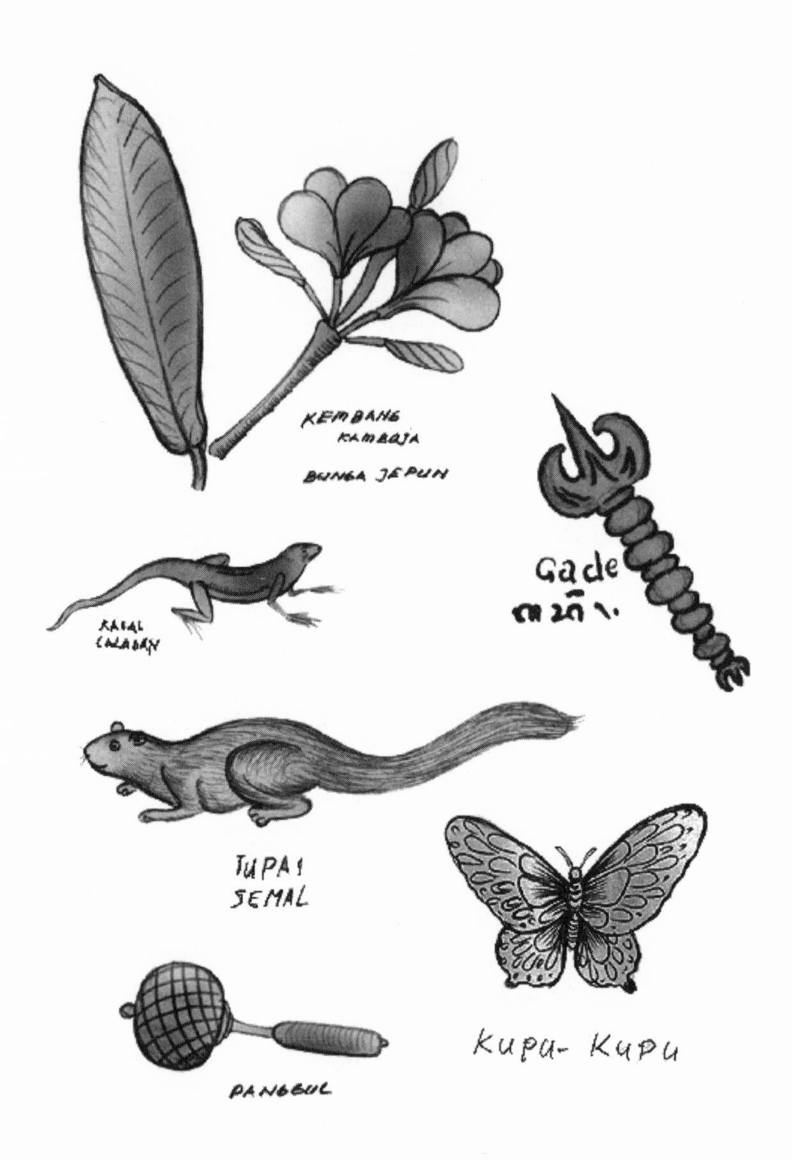
KEMBANG
KAMBOJA
BUNGA JEPUN
Gade
TUPAI
SEMAL
Kupu- Kupu
PANGGUL

GLOSSARY

The non-English words that appear in this book and glossary are Indonesian, Sanskrit, or Balinese. Eddie's and Nick's made-up word combinations are also indicated.

amok: crazy, insane, as in "run amok."

anak: child.

"Apa itu?": "What's that?" Probably the first sentence we learned.

api: fire.

arak: Balinese rice brandy wine.

Ardja: an operatic-style musical comedy. One of the most popular of the Balinese dance forms.

Arjuna: the most noble of princes seen in the shadow play and dances of Bali. The quintessential Balinese hero.

bagus: good, beautiful, pretty, fine, excellent.

bale banjar: the roofed pavilion where the banjar meets.

balian: traditional healer or medicine man, some consult ancient lontar texts before preparing herbal remedies, others are mediums and channel the ancestors while in trance.

banjar: the ruling organization in the village. The bale banyar is the building where council meetings are held and where the gamelan practices. It's a communal meeting hall.

Baris: the Balinese warrior dance which may be danced by one or many, usually with a ritual weapon.

Barong: the mythical lion-like beast, a protective and good creature. The body appears like a lion, and the face mask varies. The face may be a tiger, wild boar, elephant, lion, pig, or unknown animal.

"Belum, nanti": "Not yet," "Maybe later," "Catch you later."

betel-nut: mildly stimulating drug which creates red saliva that stains the teeth.

bemo: a small truck with two rows of seats in the back for passengers.

Bima: one of the five Pandawa brothers from the *Mahabharata,* appears in the shadow play as well as many of the dance dramas of Bali and Java.

bioskop: the cinema, movies, or a motion picture camera.

bulan: moon or month

chakras: literally "wheel." Refers to spinning wheel-like energy centers in the body. Also "wheel-like" weapons used by gods and demons, such as the Wheel of the Cosmos, which destroys all illusion.

dalang: the Balinese shadow puppet master.

"Dari mana?": "Where are you from?," a frequent question asked by all.

Delem: a clown in the Balinese shadow play belonging to the family of the bad.

drama gila: our word for going crazy before an audience.

drama makan: our word for eating before an audience.

dukun: traditional healer or medicine man, some consult

ancient lontar texts before preparing herbal remedies, others are mediums and channel the ancestors while in trance.

durian: a popular fruit in Bali with a snake-like skin and unusually strong smell.

gamelan: the Balinese orchestra. Also a gender, the individual instrument.

gangsa: a gender. A gamelan instrument.

genders: the metallaphones used to accompany the shadow play.

gila: mad, insane.

Gunung Agung: the highest volcano in Bali, 10,300 feet high.

homestay or losmen: a small hotel, usually centered around someone's home, where travelers may stay cheaply.

jackfruit: a popular fruit in Bali.

kabaya: a woman's blouse.

kaja: a cardinal direction in Bali, toward the mountains where the gods live. The direction varies, depending on where you are.

kawan: friend, comrade, companion.

"Kawan sakit:": "Your friend is sick."

kawi: an ancient, religious language found in the lontar books, and spoken by the heroes or gods in shadow plays and dance dramas.

kayon: the Tree of Life puppet which can also be used to symbolize many other natural things like mountains, boulders, or fire.

kein: a wide sash which goes around the waist. Formal dress for temple ceremonies.

kelod: a cardinal direction in Bali, toward the sea, home of the demons. The direction varies, depending on where you are.

"Kemana": "where", "to what place?"

kopi susu: Balinese coffee with milk.

kreteks: the sputtering, sweet-smelling clove cigarettes found everywhere in Bali.

kris: the mystical, sacred Balinese dagger with a wavy blade that has great magical power.

kulkul: a signal drum carved from a hollow log used to signal or summon temple and community events.

leyaks: Balinese witches, or one who practices black magic and is able to transform themselves into another creature or animal.

lontar: palm leaves on which Balinese sacred texts are scratched. The book is bound between bamboo boards.

lontong: steamed rice wrapped in a banana leaf.

losmen or homestay: a small hotel, usually centered around someone's home, where travelers may stay cheaply.

"Ma'af kan sekali": an expression of regret, "I'm very sorry, forgive me."

mandala: a geometric motif and images endowed with magic power. Often the point of departure for a system of meditation, the aim of which is a mystic union with the supreme unity.

mandi: bath.

mantras: chants, sequences of mystical syllables designed to evoke vibrations in the body and connect one with transcendental states of awareness.

maya: illusion; a Sanskrit word meaning illusion, the impermanence of human-perceived reality.

"Minta wang": "Give me money," an expression used by children.

mengerti: understand

metallaphone: a class of musical instrument. A xylophone or gamelan instrument with metal keys that are struck with mallets.

mie goreng: fried noodles and vegetables.

mudra: religious and symbolic hand gestures used by priests during temple ceremonies and during meditation. Also seen in Buddhist and Hindu sculptures and paintings of Buddhas and gods.

Merdah: a good servant clown in the shadow play.

"Nanti": "Wait." "Later."

nasi goreng: fried rice and vegetables.

Nipas: a made-up affectionate nickname meaning "thin" instead of the name *Nicholas,* which the Balinese painters cannot pronounce.

obat: medicine.

odalan: the anniversary of a temple accompanied by special ceremonies. Could occur every 210 days if calculated by the Balinese calendar.

pandai: clever, skilled.

panggul: the wooden mallet which strikes the metal keys on gamelan instruments.

pedanda: high priest of the Brahmana caste. Could be a man or woman.

pemangku: lay priest and temple custodian of the Sudra caste.

"Permisi": an expression that one asks the host so he or she may be excused. Used when standing or walking in front of someone.

Poste Restante (Italian): the general post office where someone without an address may receive mail.

Ramayana: the most popular Hindu epic poem which is performed in just about every Balinese drama form. The story centers around the heroic Rama who saves his wife, Sita, who was kidnapped by the demon, King Rawana.

Rangda: literally means "widow." The witch of the graveyard representing the dark, shadow forces in human nature.

reyong: an instrument of overturned bowls played by four men.

rumah ketjil: small room, toilet.

rumah sakit: sick room, mental hospital

rupiah: Indonesian currency.

sadhu: beggars, religious renunciants found in India.

sakti: mystical energy and power which emanates from a carnal embrace with a god and is incarnated in a female body. Also female energy.

sakit: sick.

sakit kepala: headache.

"Salamat pagi": "good morning."

"Salamat sore": "good late afternoon."
sambal: a condiment prepared with hot pepper.

sanghyang: a sacred purification trance dance ceremony with young girls as the dancers. Sometimes features men who ride prop-horses or turn into animal spirits.

Sanghyang Widhi: the single Balinese deity that embodies all manifestations into an all-powerful one God.

Sangut: one of the clowns in the shadow play. One of the good servants.

saput: material which is wrapped around the waist before entering a temple or religious ceremony.

sarong: the tourist or popular name for the woven or batik material that both men and women wear from their waists to the ground.

saté: chicken or pork shish-kebabs.

Schmoo (American slang): a 1960's Al Capp cartoon character that is shaped like a white bowling pin and has the ability to reproduce itself.

Semar: the mythical sage from the shadow play. One of the oldest of the characters.

sendiri: alone, self.

shakti or sakti: the magical quality of sacred items, or a person's magical and spiritual power.

silakan: please

stupa: the mound-shaped roof and five-tiered structure associated with Buddhist temples. Each tier represents various aspects of Buddhist thought.

tantric: a form of mystical practices from *Tantra*, a vast body of secret religious texts largely devoted to the exaltation of the Goddess, which suggest feminine counterparts to the Buddha. These divinities represent the active aspect of their masculine counterpart. The unification of the pair is symbolized by the sexual act.

"Terima kasih": "Thank you."

"Tidak bagus": "Not good."

"Tidak besar": "It can't be done!" No.

"Tidak senang": "I don't like it."

"Tidak tau": "I don't know."

tingklik: a bamboo percussive instrument.

tidur: sleep.

tjetjaks: small lizards which make a large sound like their name.

Topeng: the masked dance drama of Bali.

vajra: represents lightning. Also a weapon of the Hindu divinity Indra: A legend tells of the Buddha who took the symbol from Indra to make a Buddhist emblem of it, symbolizing the victorious power of Buddhist law. Also mystic truth, wisdom.

warung: stands along the streets or village paths which serve tea, sweets, and snacks.

wayang kulit: the shadow play using carved, leather puppets.